just
jazz

The Faithgirlz! ™ *Bible*
Faithgirlz!™ *Backpack Bible*
My Faithgirlz!™ *Journal*

The Blog On Series

Grace Notes (Book One)
Love, Annie (Book Two)
Storm Rising (Book Four)

The Sophie Series

Sophie's World (Book One)
Sophie's Secret (Book Two)
Sophie and the Scoundrels (Book Three)
Sophie's Irish Showdown (Book Four)
Sophie's First Dance? (Book Five)
Sophie's Stormy Summer (Book Six)
Sophie Breaks the Code (Book Seven)
Sophie Tracks a Thief (Book Eight)
Sophie Flakes Out (Book Nine)
Sophie Loves Jimmy (Book Ten)
Sophie Loses the Lead (Book Eleven)
Sophie's Encore (Book Twelve)

Nonfiction

No Boys Allowed: Devotions for Girls
Girls Rock: Devotions for You
Chick Chat: More Devotions for Girls
Shine On, Girl!: Devotions to Keep You Sparkling

Check out www.faithgirlz.com

faiThGirLz!

just jazz

DANDI DALEY MACKALL

zonder**kidz**

ZONDERVAN.COM/
AUTHOR**TRACKER**

The children's group of Zondervan

www.zonderkidz.com

Just Jazz
Copyright © 2006 by Dandi Daley Mackall
Illustrations © 2006 by The Zondervan Corporation

Requests for information should be addressed to:
Zonderkidz, 5300 Patterson Ave. SE
Grand Rapids, Michigan 49530

Library of Congress Cataloging-in-Publication Data

Mackall, Dandi Daley.
Just Jazz / by Dandi Daley Mackall.
        p. cm. -- (Faithgirlz)
        Summary: Artistic Jasmine "Jazz" Fletcher tries to find a way to convince her skeptical parents that art for her is not just an expensive hobby but an important part of life.
        ISBN-13: 978-0-310-71095-0 (softcover)
        ISBN-10: 0-310-71095-2 (softcover)
        [1. Artists–Fiction. 2. Self-perception–Fiction. 3. Interpersonal relations–Fiction. 4. Parent and child–Fiction. 5. Christian life–Fiction.] I. Title. II. Series.
        PZ7.M1905 Ju 2006
        [[Fic]–dc22

                                                    2005037178

Art direction: Laura Maitner-Mason
Illustrator: Julie Speer
Cover design: Karen Phillips
Interior design: Pamela J.L. Eicher
Interior composition: Ruth Bandstra

Illustrations used in this book were created in Adobe Illustrator.
The body text for this book is set in Cochin Medium.

Printed in the United States of America

06 07 08 09 10 • 10 9 8 7 6 5 4 3 2 1

So we fix our eyes not on what is seen, but on what is unseen. For what is seen is temporary, but what is unseen is eternal.

— 2 Corinthians 4:18

1

Jazz Fletcher stormed outside, slamming the door behind her. But the giant cedar door to the Fletcher mansion didn't slam. It *swooshed* shut.

Great, Jazz thought, as she stared up at the gray, cloudless sky. *It's not enough that everyone in my house is against me. The house itself hates me.*

She shook her head to try to get rid of her mother's last words — Jazz's mother always got the last word: "Jazz, you'll have time to play with your paints and things in the summer. The school year is for *real* classes."

Jazz and her parents had argued about her art so often, Jazz could have performed both sides of the argument word for word. But it didn't matter. She was going to be an artist, no matter what they thought.

Jazz took off for Gracie's cottage, walking so fast that the crisp October air tickled her nostrils. Grace Doe had started a website, *That's What You Think!,* where she'd blogged her observations about people. Now a team of girls ran the site, and Jazz's job was, of course, art design — graphics and an occasional cartoon. Jazz figured she'd be late to their weekly meeting, thanks to her mother.

Jazz was almost to the cottage when she noticed a waft of smoke, filtered and flavored, through someone's chimney. She sniffed the air and thought she could even smell the color of the red orange maple leaves, softer than the yellow ginkgos still clinging to branches. She'd have given anything to have her canvas and paints right now. She'd capture it all, including the hint of gasoline from a mower. She would take the unseen smells and turn them into a masterpiece.

A horn honked.

Jazz realized she was standing in the middle of the road. It wasn't a busy street. But the red Honda obviously didn't have time for teenaged artists. She took in one last breath and trotted to the sidewalk.

What if the picture she'd had in her head seconds ago, the painting of autumn smells, could have been her masterpiece? The one thing that would make everybody, especially her art-hating parents, sit up and take notice? Already the vision faded, the reds becoming less red, the umber washing to pale yellow.

She walked the rest of the way to Gracie's cottage. Jazz was pretty sure a couple of her friends would have given her grief for throwing in with Gracie's group, if they'd known about it. But *That's What You Think!* was anonymous. Big Lake High was "Typical High," and Gracie made up funny names for everybody she blogged about. And anyway, being part of the blog was one of the few good things going on in Jazz's life right now, not that she'd ever say it out loud.

Jazz knocked on the cottage door, then walked on in. "Anybody home?" She inhaled the lilac and musty smell of the cottage. The place belonged to Gracie's mom, who was almost always traveling in Europe. Gracie had started trying to get the group together Saturday mornings, and this was their base of operation.

"You're late," Gracie mumbled, taking Jazz's jacket when she shrugged out of it.

"Guilty," Jazz replied.

Gracie was pretty straight-up. What you saw was what you got.

Jazz appreciated that. She could imagine doing an abstract portrait of Grace Doe. Instead of painting Gracie's short, straight, blonde hair and big, hazel eyes in a glorified snapshot, the way their art teacher encouraged them to paint, Jazz would center the abstract on a tiny scar above Gracie's right eyebrow. The scar was so thin and short that Jazz knew nobody ever noticed it, except her. But to Jazz, the scar said everything. It symbolized a pain inside of Gracie, something caused by her parents' divorce, when her mom had left Gracie with her dad. That scar seemed to have healed over too, more or less. Jazz had asked Gracie about the scar once, and it was nothing more than a cut from an old bicycle accident. Not to Jazz.

Mick, Gracie's little stepsis and the blog's technical guru, was already clicking away at the computer keys. "Hey, Jazz!" she called.

"Hey yourself, Munch." Jazz handed Mick the cartoon she'd drawn earlier in the week and leaned on the back of Mick's chair. As always, Mick took the drawing without looking or showing it to anybody, flipped it over, and placed it in the scanner. In seconds, she had the colorized sketch uploaded. Jazz and Gracie crowded at the edges of the screen.

"That rocks!" Mick exclaimed, adjusting the scanned image.

"Excellent," Gracie agreed.

Jazz brushed off the praise, but she clung to it on the inside. It felt good to have somebody appreciate her work for a change. She changed the subject before Gracie had a chance to "read" her. The girl was an expert in observing gestures and picking up on signs of emotion, little things nobody else would notice. "So why aren't Storm and Annie here?"

"I don't know about Storm. Annie had cheerleading or something," Mick explained. "But she dropped off her 'Professor Love' column."

"Let's see it." Jazz reached over and jiggled the mouse to wake the screen from sleep mode.

Gracie threw herself in front of the computer, blocking the screen. "Okay. Jazz, promise you won't get mad. Storm saw my blog, and she's okay with it."

"Gracie! You wrote about us again?" Jazz accused.

"True," Gracie admitted. "But Storm is still 'New Girl.' And I changed your name to 'Monet.'"

Jazz nudged Gracie away from the screen and started with her blog. "Should have changed my name to 'Van Gogh.' He never sold anything while he was alive either."

● ● ● ● ● ● ● ● ● ● ● ● ● ● ● ● ● ● ●

THAT'S WHAT YOU THINK!
by Jane
OCTOBER 4
SUBJECT: A CONVERSATION WITH BODIES

So last week in art, New Girl got paired with Pastel Princess when we had to paint each other. Princess is a freshman, like New Girl, but there end the similarities. Without uttering a word to each other, their unspoken conversation went like this:

Pastel Princess:	*Clasped hands. ["Cool!"]*
New Girl:	*Angled her upper body thirty degrees away from Princess. ["You've got to be kidding."]*
Princess:	*Squared herself to face New Girl. ["You start, okay? Will you, huh?"]*
New Girl:	*Rubbed forehead ["Oh, man! Why me?"], crossed legs ["Let's get this over with."], and then placed palms down on desk. ["Okay. This is how it's going to be. Got it?"]*
Princess:	*Pulled arms and elbows into body. ["Whatever you say."]*
New Girl:	*Lifted face and chin. ["You got that right."]*

The body language between Monet and Perfect Guy was much shorter, but every bit as enlightening:

Monet:	*Arms crossed, with elbows high and pointed out. ["This is too cruel, even for the art teacher. No way I'm painting this guy."]*
Perfect Guy:	*Inhaled, balloon-like, keeping his profile to Monet. ["I, of course, shall begin. Watch how I do it and be enlightened."]*

"So who's Perfect Guy?" Mick asked.

Jazz had no trouble with that one. "Paul Brown," she answered. Gracie had nailed Paul. "His mother has an office on Dad's floor at Spiels Corporation. My parents think Paul Brown is perfect. So does Paul, for that matter. So do Paul's parents."

The second she said it, something twisted in her chest.
Paul's parents did think their son was perfect. They came to
every open house and fussed over each sketch or painting or
sculpture Paul had on display.

Jazz walked off to the kitchen for a glass of water. She
didn't want Gracie to see her, to *read* her, to read her thoughts
by her gestures or expression. Not right now. Because what
Jazz was thinking was what it must feel like to be Paul, to
have your parents love everything you do in art. To have your
parents think you were perfect.

It was something Jazz knew she would never have.

2

Mick gave up her seat behind the computer, and Jazz took charge. She scrolled through Annie's "Professor Love" column. Annie's answers to the "Dear Professor Love" questions were so tight. Jazz still had trouble reconciling the witty Professor Love with cheerleader Annie. This week Annie had answered questions about break-ups and group dating. Then she'd done something Jazz *didn't* like. She'd gotten serious and challenged readers to think about the way God loved them. Gracie had been doing the same kind of thing in her blogs. Jazz didn't want to talk about God on the website, or anywhere else, for that matter. But she held her peace . . . for now.

She scrolled through to reread her favorite Q and A. It was from someone calling herself "Dr. Love."

. . . .
THAT'S WHAT YOU THINK!

Dear Professor Love,

I thought I'd give your readers some advice that u don't seem 2 no. I show my boyfriend how much i love him by

*sending him cards all the time. I buy half a dozen greeting
cards and have them on hand, so all I have 2 do is sign
one and drop it in the mail or stick it in his locker 4 a
surprise. Can't believe u haven't thought of this yourself.
And u call yourself a professor of love?*

— Dr. Love

What's up Doc?

*How kind of you to send your input. (Did you buy it at
a store in advance and mail?) You show your love with
cards, huh? The kind with those pre-written greetings
inside? I hope you add something of your own, maybe
something like: "I'm not clever enough to come up with
anything cool to say on my own. So here's what a stranger
said about nobody in particular. What he says."*

Love, Professor Love

Jazz thought she heard the front door open, but they were
all laughing so hard, she wasn't sure.

"No fair laughing without me!" Storm Novelo breezed into
the living room. She was wearing a long dress that would
have been perfect for a Medieval Renaissance fair. Her
straight, black hair hung to her waist. A freshman, like Jazz,
Storm had only lived in Big Lake a few weeks, but she was
already as popular as Annie. You couldn't help but like her.
She was a force of nature. Jazz thought an abstract of Storm
would take every color in her palette.

"Nice you could make it, Storm," Gracie said with her usual
sarcasm. But even she couldn't help smiling at Storm.

"Hey, Storm!" Mick called. "If you've got your disk, I'll load it."

Jazz returned the computer chair to Mick. She grinned at Storm. "So, don't we rate one of the famous Storm excuses for why you're so late?"

Storm returned the grin. "Sorry. Okay. How about, I had to stop at the ATM, and I couldn't decide whether I wanted instructions in English or Spanish. And when I finally chose Spanish, I got pesos, which don't work at the DQ, so I had to go inside and get dollars, and the whole thing was a big mess."

"Well, that's more like it," Jazz said.

"Got it!" Mick called.

Jazz squeezed in with the others and read Storm's blog:

. . . .
THAT'S WHAT YOU THINK!

DIDYANOSE:

Did you know?

- *In Russia, teens almost always date in groups, not to movies, but to coffeehouses.*
- *In Japan, teens don't date at all until they're out of high school.*
- *In Finland, large groups for most dates — that's the norm (probably so they keep each other warm).*
- *Most teens don't date in Afghanistan. In fact, a lot of them don't even meet each other until they're married!*
- *In Iran, it's against the law for teens to date.*

"Pretty tight," Jazz commented.

"So what's everybody doing for next week?" Grace asked. "Annie's all set for her column." Gracie held up a fistful of printouts. "These are just a fraction of the emails addressed to Professor Love."

"How about mysteries? Like that things aren't always what they appear to be?" Storm asked it as if she were crammed with so much information she had to write about it. "Like how you'd think adults had more bones than babies, right? But babies are born with 300–350 bones, and grown-ups only have 206, and half of those are in feet and hands. Or, sneezes! I mean, you can't actually see a sneeze. So you'd never guess it, but sneezes can travel at one hundred miles an hour! And don't get me started on coughs!"

Gracie nodded, expressionless, but Jazz could tell she really liked the idea. "Works for me. I always blog about things most people don't see or pick up on. Annie could focus on questions from girls who discover their dream guys aren't what they appeared to be. Or from guys who finally see through their so-called perfect women."

Mick had been typing while they talked. She grinned up at them now. Jazz believed that Mick was one of the good ones. Mick and Jazz's little brother, Ty, had been best buddies for years. "I thought this verse might fit next week's blog," Mick began. "'So we fix our eyes not on what is seen, but on what is unseen. For what is seen is temporary, but what is unseen is eternal, 2 Corinthians 4:18.' What do you think? Is it okay?"

The others studied the screen, but Jazz walked away and stared out the window at the shagbark hickory in the front lawn. She loved the scruffy bark that looked like a warm, winter coat.

"Too cool, Munch!" Gracie exclaimed."I don't know how you always find the exact right verse."

Storm didn't comment. Jazz thought Storm might feel the way she did. Jazz had voiced her opinion before, but she was going to say it again. "Are you guys sure you want Bible stuff on the website? No offense, Mick, but that's not what people come to read. You might turn some people off." Truth was, Jazz didn't care if it turned people off or not. It turned *her* off. "Sometimes people have had too much bad stuff happen in their lives to believe in God."

Like having a brother shot in a drive-by before you even got a chance to know him.

Jazz had only been a baby when DC died. She didn't even remember the old Cleveland neighborhood, and her parents wouldn't talk about it. But her brother's death had changed them. They'd both gone back to school and done everything they could to get to the suburbs. Mom worked her way up as a stockbroker, and Dad became a VP at Spiels.

"We know where you're coming from, Jazz," Gracie said. "But God believes in people even if they don't believe in him. Let's just leave it for now, okay?"

It wasn't okay with Jazz, but she let it go.

Gracie glanced at her watch. "I've gotta bounce. If I'm not at the store in fifteen minutes, I'll lose my bagging job."

"Ooh — me too!" Storm cried. "I tried to get a later shift, but no-go."

Mick grabbed her Indians jacket off the computer chair. "I promised Annie's mom I'd help out at the shop today."

Jazz always felt weird when the others talked about their weekend jobs. She would have loved to work at the supermarket with Storm and Gracie, or with Annie and Mick at Sam's Sammich Shop, the hangout owned by Annie's mom. But Jazz's parents went postal whenever Jazz brought it up. They said she didn't need to work. And if she wanted to, she could do something that would help her "get ahead," like starting training at Spiels, Dad's corporation.

Jazz would rather pull out her eyelashes.

She took her time walking back home. The Fletchers, of course, lived in the biggest house in the new development, where the most expensive homes in Big Lake were built. The two-story mansion wasn't what Jazz would have picked. It had no character. Her mother had hired the best interior decorators from Cleveland, and their living room had made the art section of *Cleveland Magazine*. But that's what the house felt like, inside and out. A magazine house, not a home.

One thing about it Jazz did love. Her bedroom was big enough to double as her art studio, which was where she intended to spend the rest of the day. She was in the middle of two art projects, neither of them for art class. One was an almost-finished collage of things she'd rescued from the school dumpster. The other was the beginning of a sculpture she was making to reflect the sounds of a busy Cleveland intersection.

Jazz unlocked the front door, and Kendra came running. "Jasmine, I missed you!" Kendra was thirteen, a year older than Ty, a year younger than Jazz. She attended Olympic, a special school on the north end of town, because kids were too mean to her in public school. Their parents believed Kendra would get the best education in a school that specialized in students with Down syndrome. Kendra was shorter than Jazz, but she weighed quite a bit more. Her eyes and nose were tiny, sharing space in the center of her face and dancing above big teeth and an even bigger smile. Jazz had never tried to paint or sculpt her sister because nothing could come close to capturing Kendra's spirit.

She hugged Kendra and kissed the top of her head. "No cartoons this morning?"

"Mommy made me clean my room. And Mrs. Cleaning Lady did yours all by herself except for Mommy helped her with words."

Jazz stopped breathing. *"My* room? They cleaned *my room*?"

Kendra nodded. "I cleaned my own room my own self."

Jazz tore around Kendra and took the stairs two at a time. Her mother couldn't have done this. Not again. The last time she'd "cleaned" Jazz's room six weeks' work in cut-and-paste pastels got ditched.

Jazz flung open her door. The room smelled like lemon cleaner and ammonia. The wood floor looked polished and new.

And Jazz's art projects, her materials, her sculpture, the collage board — they were all gone.

3

Jazz stormed down the stairs. "Mother!" She almost bumped into Ty, who was dragging his bat up the stairs.

"Hey, Jasmine," Ty called. "Did you see Mick?"

"Not now, Ty." Jazz dodged her little brother and rounded the corner to her mother's study. Her mom worked nearly every Saturday of their lives. Why couldn't she have been off selling office buildings or negotiating land deals today, instead of ruining Jazz's life?

Mom's study was at the far end of the downstairs wing, off the parlor, the quietest spot in the house. The door was closed. Jazz broke the knock-first rule and barged in. Mom was sitting at her long, oak desk, surrounded by wooden file cabinets, under a wall of shelves that held law books and notebook binders.

She frowned up at Jazz. Even around her own house, Tosha Fletcher looked and dressed the part of a high-powered stockbroker. The jacket of her navy pantsuit was buttoned, and her makeup looked perfect. Jazz knew she got her slender build from her mom, but she would never have Mom's sophistication. Jazz wasn't sure she wanted it.

"Jasmine? Did you knock?" She slid off her small, black-framed glasses with one hand and leaned back in the leather desk chair.

"Did *you*?" Jazz snapped. "Did you knock when you sneaked into my room while I was gone and destroyed everything I've been — ?"

"Don't use that tone in this house," her mother interrupted evenly.

For the hundredth time, Jazz wished she lived in a home where people yelled on the outside instead of yelling on the inside. She took a deep breath because she knew she'd never get anywhere this way.

"Where are my art projects?" she asked, her words calm, but brittle.

"I don't know what you mean," her mother answered. "If you mean that junk you had cluttering your room, it's where junk belongs. In the trash."

"How could you do that?" Jazz tried to stare through her mother, to the place where a heart should have been. "I've been working for weeks on those projects."

"Jazz, I threw away garbage, and that was all. An old tennis shoe? Chalk? Dried-up pens? Wadded paper? I had it hauled away. Are you trying to tell me that art class you're in makes you work with trash?"

"It wasn't for art class," Jazz said. Jazz's art teacher, Ms. Biederman, didn't understand art much better than Jazz's mother. Everything had to be traditional. That's why Jazz needed her home studio, for her real work. "It was a collage. And my sculpture? What did you do with that?"

Jazz's mom shook her head. "Sculpture? Do you mean the metal thing that was scratching your floor? Come on now, Jasmine. You're not a child. I can't let you collect scrap metal and tin foil under your bed."

"What's going on in here?"

Jazz turned to see her dad in the doorway. She hadn't heard him walk in, which was pretty amazing, since he took up the whole doorway, standing six-feet-four and weighing over 200 pounds. Alex Fletcher was a senior executive, but he looked more like an aging football player to Jazz.

"Well?" His voice was deep and solid. Once, Jazz had tried to capture Dad's voice on canvas. She'd used every shade of black and stone gray she could create, and she still hadn't gotten it.

Mom took over. "Jasmine is upset because I cleaned her room for her while she was out with friends."

Jazz wheeled back on her mother. "You wrecked my collage, and you threw away my sculpture!"

"Do we have to go through this again?" Dad asked. He lowered his gaze on Jazz, and she could tell instantly whose side he was on. And it wasn't hers. "Jasmine, why don't you do your drawings or whatever you do at school? Isn't that what that *art* class is for?" Dad couldn't even say "art class" without making it sound like basket weaving or hair braiding.

"I do work there." Jazz had to be careful not to say anything too negative about her art class. She'd had to fight to take it in the first place. And even though her art teacher didn't like anything inventive or creative, the class was better than no art class at all. "It's just that I want to work on my art at home, too. What's wrong with that?"

"Should we formulate our answers to that question alphabetically?" Mom asked.

"Tosha," Dad muttered. For a minute Jazz thought he might edge over to her side. Then he said, "Jasmine, we let you take that class."

"And I'm grateful, Dad. I am."

"Even though," Mom added, "it's the only class you're *not* getting an A in."

"Ms. B isn't open to true art," Jazz snapped before she could stop herself.

"Eleanor Brown says her son, Paul, loves that art class, *and* he's getting A's," Dad informed her.

"Proves my point," Jazz muttered.

Dad sighed. "Well, you better work it out, Jasmine, because I'm not going to have art bring down your grade point average."

Jazz wanted to stomp out of the room, but she wasn't five years old anymore. "All I want is to be able to paint and sculpt in my own room without coming home and finding everything's been thrown out."

Mom stood up from her chair and deliberately closed the giant book on her desk. "And then what, Jasmine?"

"Then I'll keep developing my art," Jazz answered, feeling herself getting sucked into the oncoming tornado.

"And?" Her mother stared at her, waiting for an answer.

"Then I'll be out of high school and can get a scholarship to a great art school."

"And?" Her mother was the most relentless human on earth.

"And I'll make a living doing something I love, art, instead of killing myself every day in a job I hate." The second she said it, Jazz knew she'd crossed the line.

"Like your mother and I do?" Dad asked in his accusing tone. "Is that what you mean?"

"I didn't say that." Jazz wanted to backtrack, but it was too late.

"Well, it won't do, Jasmine," Dad said. "You may not understand this now, but one day you will. You need to find yourself a *real* career. Paint as a hobby, if you have to. But believe me, things won't always be handed to you like they are now. You have to be able to support yourself with a *real* job, even if it isn't fun every day."

"I can do that with my art!" Jazz protested.

Her mother bit her upper lip, as if fighting for that supreme control she always had over her emotions. "Jasmine, we love you. And we'll always love anything our kids make for us. You know that. But honey, you're not going to make a living with your art. The sooner you face reality, the better. You need to plan now for your career. It's a tough world out there, especially for a black woman. You're beautiful enough to be a model, but thank heavens, you don't want to be. And you're smart enough to be a lawyer or a doctor or anything you want to be. Your father and I have worked our whole lives so you could have a good life with financial security."

"You don't think I'm good enough to be paid for my art, do you?"

"That's not what we're saying, honey," Dad explained. "Art just isn't a safe career move."

"Because I *can* make money with my art!" Jazz had earned good money once for her work. Annie's mom, Samantha Lind, had hired her to paint a beach mural on one whole wall of Sam's Sammich Shop. Jazz had been so embarrassed by the plain, realistic style of art that she'd sworn Sam and Annie to secrecy. But she'd gotten paid for the job, and they'd been happy to pay her.

"Are you talking about that thing you did at that sandwich shop, honey?" Dad asked. Jazz didn't think he'd even gone in to see it. "You can't count on always having friends with shops for you to paint."

"I can sell my paintings, my sculptures, my collages," Jazz insisted.

Mom didn't argue the point, but Jazz could see on her face how hard it was for her not to.

"If you leave my room alone, I can do all kinds of things I could sell. But I need a place to work." She was losing it now, but it was too late to stop.

"Jasmine," Dad said, like he was putting down a five-year-old who wanted to build a rocket to the moon before breakfast. "Your mother has to clean this house."

Jazz started to point out that Mrs. Bergman cleaned the house, but she caught herself in time. "This isn't fair." Yeah. It was the argument of a five-year-old, but she was so angry, it was the best she could do.

"Fair?" Mom repeated. "All right. Since we're talking about the *real* world. Let's make a *fair* business proposition."

Jazz braced herself. This was vintage Mom. Ever since Jazz could remember, her mother had made "business propositions" with her, designed to teach her daughter the ways of the *real* world. Jazz had taken most of Mom's deals, and she'd lost nearly every one.

"Jasmine," Mom continued, "here's my proposition. If you can earn money from selling your artwork, then you can have your art studio."

"Tosha?" Dad obviously didn't like where this was going. "What about her room? You hate all that stuff in her room."

"Well, then we'll turn the second guest bedroom into a studio. How's that?"

Jazz had always dreamed of annexing the room next to hers and using it for a studio. Nobody had stayed in that guest room for years. "That would be great!"

"But that's just half of the fair bargain," Mom continued, coming around the desk. "A business proposition must be fair for both sides. So, if you can make money from your art, you get your art studio in our home. In exchange, if you don't make money from your art, say, by the end of the month, then you have to agree to keep those *things* you use out of the house. And no more art classes. There are too many other courses you need to take to prepare yourself for the university."

"Fine," Jazz agreed.

Mom looked so sure of herself. "Fine." She smiled at Jazz. "And I really hope you surprise me on this one, Jasmine. Maybe I'm wrong. Maybe it's time we both find out."

A faint knock sounded on the study door, even though it was still open. Ty stood there, looking sheepish, a ball in one hand, a glove in the other. "Anybody want to play ball?"

Jazz knew how much it had taken for Ty to come in and rescue her. He hated conflict.

Dad turned to Ty. "No. But I think we're done here."

Jazz hurried out before Mom could add conditions to her business proposition, like she did sometimes. As Jazz passed Ty in the doorway, she whispered, "Thanks." Then she dashed to her room, shut the door, and stared at the empty corner where her art projects had been.

Someone tapped on her door.

"It's open," she snapped.

Kendra tiptoed in, hands behind her back and a big grin on her face. "I got something for you."

The last thing Jazz felt like doing was smiling, but she forced herself to. "You do?"

From behind her back, Kendra whisked out a piece of jagged-edged notebook paper and handed it to Jazz. "It's for *you*!"

Jazz took the paper. Kendra had drawn a stick figure. It was the same picture she always drew — one pencil line for the body, two for the legs, two for arms, each with seven fingers, and a lopsided circle head. "It's amazing, Kendra! Thanks, honey." Jazz hugged her sister, then released her.

"Jasmine is all happy now?" Kendra asked, her tiny eyes widened as much as they could.

Jazz nodded.

Kendra turned on her heels and thundered down the stairs, her mission accomplished.

Jazz shut the door slowly. Then she walked to her bulletin board and tacked up the stick drawing. It joined at least twenty identical pictures, all gifts from Kendra.

As she stared at the crowd of stick figures, Jazz fought off the panic pressing at her chest, trying to get in, or trying to get out — she wasn't sure which. How was she going to make money from her art by the end of the month? Sell her abstracts? She might just as well try selling Kendra's stick figures.

4

Jazz had everything to prove and not many days to prove it. There was no time to sit around doubting her art.

She walked straight to her closet and dug out her two best pieces of finished artwork. She'd stashed them in the back, behind the power clothes Mom bought that Jazz never wore.

She pulled out a canvas and untied the string and cloth she'd wrapped it in. The painting had come to her while she'd been doing a boring painting in her art class. It hadn't taken many brain cells to copy a vase of flowers Mrs. B had set up on her desk. So while Jazz's hand had painted flowers for her teacher, her brain had imagined the *real* art she'd create at home. Every night she'd worked on her abstract.

Jazz held the canvas to her window. The painting was just as she remembered, maybe better. She'd done exactly what she'd set out to do — capture her family. A thin, straight, strong green line dominated the painting and mirrored her mother's authoritative voice. The line echoed everywhere, even going off the canvas in places. Below ran browns and oranges in broad, but controlled patterns of disappointment, her father's disappointment. Ty's line broke into pieces, pleading, touching everybody's lines, while Kendra's shocking yellows and oranges were electric. It was her family, all right. The only thing missing was Jazz.

She searched back through her closet until she found the second money-making possibility, a statue the size of her arm. She unwrapped it and studied the silver metal and clay form. She'd worked on it the same summer she painted the beach wall mural at Sam's Sammich Shop. All day she'd listened to Beach Boys music and painted what Samantha Lind had wanted her to. It wasn't great art, and she hadn't signed it, but the customers seemed to like the beach party scene.

When she was all done, she'd borrowed the Beach Boys tapes and worked on her statue in her bedroom. She'd created what, to her, was "Big Lake." Not this town in Ohio, where she'd lived almost her whole life. It was an odd name for a town that didn't have a single lake within its borders. And it was an odd name for this sculpture, which was tall, twisted, and in your face. For Jazz, it represented the unseen essence of the lake nobody else could see.

These were her best shots at making money from her artwork.

She packed them carefully into her big suitcase with wheels and pulled them out into the hall. Getting the suitcase down the stairs without making any noise wasn't easy, but she did it. Then she slipped on her jacket and stepped outside.

Ty was waiting for her. "Jasmine, you can't leave! They didn't mean it!"

Jazz grinned at her brother. Sometimes Ty could seem like an older brother, and other times, like now, he seemed a lot younger. "I'm not running away from home, Ty. I'm going to the museum on Main Street."

He fell in with her. "You mean that picture frame shop? Can I come?"

Jazz tried to talk Ty out of it, but she was kind of glad she didn't succeed. She felt pretty silly pulling a suitcase through town. At least now if she saw somebody she knew, she could hand the suitcase to Ty.

Farley's Frames was the only place in Big Lake that sold original art. Mr. Farley majored in made-to-order frames, but he also sold original paintings. Jazz visited the store at least once a week to see if anything new had come in.

A bell rang when Jazz tugged open the front door. Ty helped her lug the suitcase inside.

"Are you moving in, Jasmine?" Mr. Farley asked, leaving a customer to walk over to them. He was taller than Jazz's dad, but bone thin. He reminded Jazz of the kind of character you'd find in a nursery rhyme. His eyes were deep set and hollow, something Van Gogh or Picasso would have liked painting. Jazz liked him, although they'd gotten off to a bad start. She'd been pretty blunt when she'd checked out his first batch of oil paintings. They liked some of the same things, but he was still pretty conservative.

Jazz introduced Ty to Mr. Farley and then unzipped the suitcase. "I brought you something, Mr. Farley."

"Oh?"

Her hands shook just a little as she unwrapped the sculpture and handed it to him. "I thought you might want to sell this, and we could split the money." She couldn't look at him as she waited for his reaction.

"You did this?" He rubbed his chin. "It's interesting, Jasmine. But I'm afraid I can't see anyone around here purchasing it."

She told herself that the sculpture had been a long shot. The only figures in the store were trendy, Native American pieces. "That's kind of what I thought. Here." She handed him her painting. She wished she'd titled it, maybe taken the time to get a nameplate. Why hadn't she thought to frame it first?

"Jasmine, you have talent," he said, staring at the picture.

Jazz had waited a long time to hear those words. *Jasmine, you have talent.* She wished her dad could have been here to hear this. And her mom. "Thanks, Mr. Farley," she managed.

"Um hum. The colors are unusual, but right somehow. And the lines. I like the movement. But . . . ."

Please don't say "but."

"But it just wouldn't do any good, not here." He shook his head and handed the painting back to her. "I'm sorry."

"You wouldn't have to pay me anything until it sold," she tried.

He kept shaking his head. "I have a warehouse full of paintings I'd like to showcase in the store. But I can't put another one up until one of these sells. I just can't display one I know won't sell."

"Sure looks pretty to me," Ty said. Jazz had almost forgotten her brother was there. "If I had any money, I'd buy it on the spot!"

Mr. Farley smiled down at Ty. "I'll bet you would, son." He turned to Jazz. "I'm sorry it didn't work out, Jasmine."

There was nothing else she could do. "Thanks, Mr. Farley. No big deal. I just thought . . . well, never mind." She packed the painting and sculpture into the suitcase and zipped it shut. Then she tried to look as if her world weren't falling apart.

The suitcase felt twice as heavy dragging it out of the store as it had dragging it in. What had made her believe anyone would want to buy her art? What if her mother was right? Jazz didn't want to think about a future without art.

"Hey! What are you guys up to?"

Jazz dropped her end of the suitcase and turned to see Mick and Gracie walking toward them.

"Hi, Mick!" Ty called, wrestling the suitcase on end.

"Don't say anything, Ty!" Jazz whispered. She took the suitcase from him and stretched out the pull handle.

Gracie walked up and thumped the suitcase. "So, what is it? Stolen picture frames? Amazing you didn't get caught."

"Funny," Jazz said. "Just some old stuff from my closet. I thought you were working at the supermarket."

"They let me off a little early," Gracie answered, still studying the suitcase.

"Ty," Mick said, "want to play ball?"

Ty glanced at Jazz, as if asking her permission.

"Go," she said.

Mick and Ty took off at a run, probably racing. Mick could hold her own against Jazz's brother, in a race and in baseball. Ty said she was the best pitcher on the middle school team, an all-guy's team, except for Mick.

"Where are you headed?" Jazz asked, hoping Gracie wouldn't go back to the topic of the suitcase.

"Sam's. Why don't you come with me?" Gracie walked ahead, in the direction of Sam's Sammich Shop.

Jazz started to refuse. She wasn't the social type. On the other hand, she sure didn't feel like going home. The last thing she needed was for Mom to see her dragging in her newly rejected art pieces. Finally, she followed Gracie down the sidewalk. They walked in silence, although Gracie frowned back at the suitcase a couple of times.

When they were almost to Sam's, Gracie said, "Something tells me that suitcase isn't carrying old clothes from your closet."

Jazz shrugged. She hadn't exactly said it had old clothes in it. You couldn't fool Gracie Doe that easily anyway. Jazz hurried into the shop to the very back booth, where she slid the suitcase under the table.

Beach Boys music played from the jukebox. Jazz caught a few kids staring at her, but they went back to their fries and ice cream.

Gracie took the seat across from her in the booth, and Annie came over seconds later. Everything about Annie Lind screamed "cute." She had her mom's auburn hair and big, blue eyes. Guys loved Annie. Gracie's blog name for Annie, "Bouncy Perky Girl" said it all.

"Hey, guys!" Annie pulled out a pad and pencil, just like a real waitress. "Want something?"

"How about Ice Cream à la Mick?" Jazz suggested. Mick spent so much time helping out at Sam's that she'd invented her own flavor of ice cream.

"Make it two," Gracie agreed.

"I'll make it three," Annie said, pocketing her waitress pad. "The crowd's thinned, and Granny's helping with the counter. Back in a sec."

Jazz heard Storm's squeal before she saw her. Storm Novelo burst into the shop and joined the Beach Boys in the middle of "Fun, Fun, Fun," crooning the last line of the chorus, "'til her daddy takes the T-bird away." She was still in her medieval dress. Jazz wondered how that had gone over at Big Lake Foods.

Storm danced across the floor to their booth. She scooted Jazz over. "This is so not fair!" she complained to Gracie. "You got off early, and I had to stay every single boring minute of my shift!"

"That's because they like your company better than mine," Gracie explained.

"Don't be whack!" Storm said.

Gracie had worked at Big Lake Foods a lot longer than Storm had, but Jazz guessed Gracie was telling the truth. Everybody loved Storm Novelo.

"I'm starving!" Storm gazed around the room. "Annie! Stop flirting and bring ice cream!"

Annie had gotten sidetracked on her way to the kitchen. She was sitting at a table with three guys, including Stan Lowry, her latest love interest, a nice guy this time. Annie made a face at Storm, then hopped up and disappeared into the kitchen. When she came out, she was carrying a tray with four dishes of ice cream. Gracie slid over to make room for her.

Jazz ate her ice cream while the others talked about school and the blog.

Annie's foot bumped the suitcase. "What's that?" She ducked under the table and pulled out Jazz's suitcase.

Jazz reached for it. "It's nothing. Leave it there."

Annie ignored her and slid out of the booth for a better look. "Why did you bring your suitcase in here?"

Storm scooted out of the booth, too. "What's in it? Is it yours, Jazz?"

"It's just some stuff I'm working on." Jazz wanted to grab the suitcase and run. But run where? Home? She wasn't ready for home. Not yet.

"Can we see?" Storm didn't wait for an answer. With the flick of her wrist, she unzipped the bag.

"Wait!" Jazz protested. But she wasn't fast enough. Storm already had the sculpture in her hands, and Annie was unwrapping the canvas.

"What is it?" Annie asked. She held the painting as far away from her as she could, as if it contained one of those magic pictures and the real image would show up at any moment. "It's ... I really like the colors, Jazz." She said it like she meant it. At least Jazz thought she did. But there was no mistaking the puzzled expression on Annie's face.

"This is cool." Storm set the sculpture on the table. "How'd you do it?"

"Scraps," Jazz answered. She knew Annie and Storm were only trying to be nice. They'd be the first to admit that they weren't really into art.

"Cool," Storm said again.

"Storm!" Annie set down the painting next to Jazz's sculpture and grabbed Storm's arm. "Cody's here."

Storm had gone to homecoming with Cody, but Jazz didn't think they'd gone out since. He pulled up a chair at Stan's table.

Jazz knew the girls wanted to go say hi to the guys, but didn't want to dump friends to do it. "Hey, Gracie," Jazz said. "I've got an idea. Why don't we send Annie and Storm over there to say hey to Cody and Stan for us." She grinned at Annie. "Would you mind?"

Annie grinned back. "We don't need to go over there," she said. "We were with you guys first."

"Go," Gracie seconded.

"You sure?" Storm asked.

"We're sure," Jazz promised. The sooner they left, the sooner she could stash her art back into the suitcase ... where it apparently belonged.

Jazz reached for her painting, but Gracie already had it. Jazz watched as Gracie frowned at the canvas. She held it up to the light, examined it up close and at a distance. Finally, she said almost in a whisper, "Jazz, this is amazing."

Jazz knew Gracie well enough to know that she couldn't fake compliments the way Annie and Storm could. "Yeah?"

Gracie nodded. "It reminds me of the one you started in art class, but tore up. Remember? When you painted Ms. B's voice? Only this one is better. Fuller. There's more going on." She turned to Jazz. "Is it somebody's voice too?"

Jazz couldn't believe Gracie got it. She nodded. "My family's. Kind of."

"Yeah!" Gracie traced her finger over Mom's green line. "This is so good, Jazz." She set it down on the table. "What were you doing with it?"

Jazz's brief good feeling burst. She took the painting and packed it away. "Trying to sell it."

"Why? Why would you want to sell it? You should save it, Jazz."

"Because if I don't, if I don't sell *something*, or make money from my art *somehow*, then I have to give it all up." And just like that, even though she didn't want to talk about it, and although she never would have planned it, Jazz told Gracie the whole story — the fight, the business proposition, the rejection at Farley's Frames, everything.

Gracie listened through the whole thing, and when Jazz stopped talking, all Gracie said was, "I'm sorry, Jazz. I'm going to be praying about this."

Jazz wished she hadn't said anything. She couldn't stand having anyone feel sorry for her. And she sure didn't want anybody praying for her. "Don't worry about it." She threw the sculpture into the suitcase without bothering to wrap it, then zipped the bag shut. She had to get out of there.

"Wait, Jazz!" Gracie called.

But Jazz was halfway out of the shop. The door slammed shut behind her as she left. She felt the slam. She could have painted it — hard, sharp-edged, final.

She could have painted it.

But why bother?

5

Monday Jazz hid in the back row of first-hour art class, sitting as far as she could from their art teacher. Ms. Biederman probably wasn't a bad person, just a bad teacher. And maybe she wasn't even a bad teacher, just a bad art teacher. Jazz had to admit that she'd learned a few things about art theory from Ms. B. But the well-dressed, carefully groomed woman probably would have been happier as a photographer. Then she could have been sure that every image looked just like its subject.

To Jazz, art meant a lot more than reproducing what everybody could see in front of them. An artist worked with what others couldn't see. Her job was to make them see the unseen, understand the *un*-understandable. That's what Jazz tried to do. And that's why she'd never gotten an A from her art teacher.

"Thanks for returning my calls." Grace Doe slid into the empty chair next to Jazz. She was dressed in black, except for the camouflage jacket.

Gracie had called at least half a dozen times since Jazz fled Sam's Sammich Shop. Jazz hadn't felt like talking, especially if Gracie tried to bring up Jesus again. She'd spent the rest of the weekend trying to figure out a way to make money with her art. "Sorry," Jazz muttered. "Things were kind of crazy at my house."

"Uh-huh." Gracie didn't sound convinced, but she didn't press it. She reached into her pack and came out with her notebook. Jazz was used to seeing Gracie take notes. Observations, she called them. Between classes Gracie could be spotted in dark hallways or leaning against her locker, watching people and jotting notes. She wrote instead of ate during lunch. Then she blogged her observations on *That's What You Think!*

Jazz glanced over at the notebook and saw three names, all sophomores, with sketchy notes under each, things like:

scratches his nose when he talks to her — nervous

hair tip-offs: fingers through hair — frustrated

hair flip — look at me!

hair twist — nervous

No wonder Gracie was so good at reading people.

Gracie shut her notebook and turned to Jazz. "We need to talk, Jazz. Annie said she'd ask her mom if they could use another mural in the shop. Storm thinks we ought to go door to door with your drawings and — "

"You told them?" Jazz couldn't believe it. She hadn't worried about spilling her problems to Gracie because she was sure it wouldn't go any further. Gracie wasn't a talker. She didn't gossip.

Gracie looked genuinely surprised. "I thought they could help. *I* couldn't think of anything. I'm sorry, Jazz. I didn't know it was a secret."

Part of Jazz was still angry, and maybe a little embarrassed, that Gracie had told Annie and Storm. But another part of her was relieved. She could use all the help she could get. And anyway, she couldn't stand seeing Gracie squirm. "Sorry," Jazz said. "I guess I just didn't think it would do any good to tell anybody. It's my problem. But it's cool of you guys to want to help."

Gracie looked relieved. She started to say something, but she didn't get a chance.

"So, you didn't even bother to save me a seat?" Storm Novelo burst into the room at the exact moment the bell rang, as if it announced her entrance. She was wearing lemon yellow tights, a very orange, very short, pleated skirt, and a shirt that was the shape and color of a large strawberry.

Every guy in the room, with the exception of Paul, offered Storm a seat. She took one on the front row in the exact center. "Okay," she said, when she'd settled in her seat. "Let the games begin!"

If anybody else had said that, Ms. Biederman would have sent them to the principal's office. Instead, she laughed and thanked Storm.

Storm could get away with anything, Jazz decided. She tried to imagine what Storm's parents were like. Storm said her family was mestizo, part Mayan and part Spanish, descended from royalty. Her parents probably supported everything she did. Jazz was pretty sure Storm was an only child, so she'd get all the attention at home, too. Yet Jazz really liked Storm. Everybody did.

"All right then," Ms. B said.

"Did anybody see that moon last night?" Storm interrupted. She didn't wait for an answer. "Perfect crescent. Exactly like lunula!"

"What's a lunula?" Bryce asked. He was the least artistic person in the class. Some of the jocks took art for an easy B. Even they could draw flowers the way Ms. B wanted them to.

"You have ten of them, Bryce, my boy!" Storm held up her hand and showed lime green fingernails, except for the white crescent of each nail. She pointed to the white of her index finger and said slowly, "*loon-yool-ah.*"

"Where do you get that stuff?" Callie asked. She was a cheerleading friend of Storm and Annie, and Jazz had a feeling she resented all the attention Storm got from guys.

Storm's face reddened. She snapped her gum and chewed hard. "I think I read it in a magazine, like at the beauty salon."

Jazz knew better. Storm was smart. She always had library books hidden in her pack, and they never had anything to do with required reading. The main reason Storm was on the blog was to give her an outlet for her trivia facts so she wouldn't have these little outbursts of knowledge in classes. Storm Novelo did not want to be thought of as smart. Jazz didn't get it. She didn't care if anybody thought she was smart or not. But she would have loved for everyone, especially her parents, to believe she was talented.

"Could we get back to class?" Paul asked.

"Good idea, Paul," Ms. B said, smiling at her perfect student. "Today we have a surprise. We're going to be doing something a bit different."

"I'll bet," Jazz muttered. Gracie elbowed her.

"Did you have something to say to the class, Jasmine?" Ms. B asked.

Jazz stared at her hands and shook her head.

"This week we'll all be drawing fish!" Ms. B said it as if she'd invented fish. She'd probably bring in photographs of fish, encyclopedias, maybe even a goldfish bowl, just so they'd all be sure to get it right.

Nobody applauded the new fish assignment, so Ms. B pressed on. "Who can explain to the class what a public art project is?"

Paul raised his hand like a good boy. "Public art is art that is accessible to any person in public places, for example, a park, a city center, a business plaza, etcetera. The NEA set up a program to supply sculptures for public places."

"So, it's like fountains?" April Kauffman asked. "Or generals on horses? Or soldiers?"

"Very good," Ms. B said. "Those are all examples of public art. But more recently, cities have taken to pursuing public art projects to decorate their cities and to raise much-needed funds. I'll bet some of you have visited cities where fiberglass animals have been painted and placed strategically around the city."

"Plop art." Jazz said it louder than she'd intended.

Gracie shot her a "shut-up" look, then resumed scribbling in her observation notebook.

"Did you say 'plop art'?" Ms. B demanded.

Jazz faced her squarely and answered, "That's what they call it. Not pop art, but plop art, because most of it is so tame — nice little statues that may make people smile, but would never require them to think."

Gracie cleared her throat and shoved her notebook where
Jazz could see it. Jazz glanced at the page and read: "Ms.
B — jaws in biting position. Head jerk. Tense mouth. Vertical
furrows above the nose and horizontal furrows over the
bridge of nose. ANGER!"

Jazz didn't back down. When she'd first heard about
public art projects, she'd been psyched. It was a great idea,
but most of the cities tied the hands of their artists and
stifled creativity. "In Washington D.C., the art committee
bought donkey and elephant statues. Get it? Democrats and
Republicans? But any artist who really tried to *say* something,
to paint or create art that would make a statement, got fired!
The officials wanted everything to be 'fun.' They ended up
calling the whole thing 'Party Animals,' which turned out to
be a good name for the project because it certainly wasn't art."

Storm glanced at Gracie, then turned back to Ms. B.
"My family's moved around a lot. I saw 'Cows on Parade'
in Chicago, 'Horse Mania' in Lexington, Kentucky,
Louisville's 'Sidewalk Derby.' And there was that 'Herd
about Buffalo' in, of course, Buffalo. Oh — and 'Moose in
the City' in Toronto, and 'Cattle Drive' in Plainview, Texas,
followed by 'WaCows' in Waco, Texas. I think Orlando had
plastic lizards. Seattle had these big ducks. Grand Rapids,
Michigan had rabbits for some reason. Maine did bears, and
Los Angeles did angels."

"That's wonderful, Storm!" Ms. B. exclaimed.

"I saw all those pigs in Cincinnati," April said. "Was that
public art?"

"It certainly was, April," Ms. B answered. "The Big Pig
Gig. Toledo used frogs. Some of you have seen the guitars in

Cleveland, I'm sure. They raised over two million dollars with 'GuitarMania' in 2002."

Kids nodded.

"Well, we're going to have our own public art project right here in Big Lake, Ohio!" Ms. B announced.

In spite of herself, Jazz felt excitement forming inside her. Big Lake had never shown any interest in the arts.

"We don't have much time," Ms. B continued. "Artists will decorate their projects in various private businesses that have donated money for materials. The work has to be done this week since judging takes place Saturday, followed by a city-wide silent auction. We would have liked to start the project last spring and have the statues on display all summer, but it took this long to get our fiberglass fish."

"Fish?" Jazz asked.

"Yes, fish." Ms. B sounded defensive. "We were able to get twelve fiberglass fish, each four feet long. The winner's fish will be moved to City Hall. The others will go to the highest bidder in silent auctions. All profit will benefit town improvement projects."

Jazz tried to think. A contest? An auction? That meant money. Money for art. What if she could win the contest? Or even make money in the auction? Her mother would have to accept that! "Do they all have to be fish?" Jazz asked. "Couldn't some of us do something else?"

Ms. B's eye twitched. Jazz saw Gracie go for her notebook again. "Not *all* of us will have a chance to participate," Ms. B explained. "Perhaps I'd better make that clear. The city has graciously given me the use of four fiberglass fish, two for each of my art classes. So only two students in this class will be allowed to decorate fish."

"Exactly what kind of fish?" Paul asked. "Lake fish, I assume?"

That was so like Paul, Jazz thought. In a minute, he'd ask Ms. B for a photograph to copy.

"Twit," Storm said.

"What?" Paul demanded.

"Twit," Storm repeated. Paul started to whine to the teacher, but Storm shut him off, as if she didn't even realize he was upset. "As in a pregnant goldfish. Could you do something like that?"

"Well ..." Ms. B seemed to be thinking it over.

"Or a father sea catfish!" Storm exclaimed. "A daddy sea catfish keeps the eggs of his young in his mouth the whole time until they're ready to hatch! He refuses to eat until his babies are born, even though that means he starves for weeks and weeks."

"Cool," April said.

"Or a giant squid! They have the biggest eyes in the whole world — the size of a basketball!" Storm was on a roll now. "Or a tiger shark! I mean, like, they start fighting while they're still in their mother's womb. The winner is the baby shark that's born. And somebody could do an orca next to the shark because those killer whales kill sharks by torpedoing up into the shark's stomach and causing it to explode! Now that's drama!"

Jazz had to laugh. She was pretty sure Storm didn't care anything about art, but her excitement was contagious. Storm hardly ever finished any of the class projects she started. But she had the creativity of an artist.

"Very interesting, Storm. Thank you. But all the fiberglass forms are the same. However, artists can paint their own designs onto the forms." Ms. B turned to face Jazz. "I only ask that our students will reflect the spirit of the project. I admit that there are no rules, but I want our class to produce art that is traditional, acceptable to all."

To Jazz, this sounded like the death warrant. But at least it would be a way to win the business proposition from her mom.

"I nominate Jazz!" Gracie shouted.

Kids turned to stare at her. Jazz tried to remember if she'd ever heard Gracie speak out in art class.

Paul obviously disapproved. "Aren't there criteria for selection of artists?"

"As a matter of fact, yes. There are a number of criteria, including talent, trustworthiness, and reliability. We have to be sure that our artists will complete the work."

Jazz had completed every art project, even the dumb ones. And she'd make her fish traditional, if that's what it took. She wanted a chance. She needed it. She almost wished she believed in God. This would have been a perfect time to pray. She pushed that thought out of her head.

"And so after long consideration, I've made my selections. Paul, you will receive one of the fiberglass fish."

"Thank you, Ms. Biederman," he answered, like he wasn't a bit surprised he'd been chosen.

Jazz sat statue-still, waiting, hoping. Storm frowned back at her, then faced front.

"Some of our talented students must realize that their not being selected isn't a judgment on their abilities. Not all artists are suited to all projects." Ms. B kept smiling at Jazz as she said this, as if the whole speech were designed just for her.

Again Storm glanced back. Jazz caught a look exchanged between Storm and Gracie, who shook her head.

Then suddenly, Storm transformed. The troubled frown disappeared, and she was gum-snapping, energetic Storm Novelo again. "I've seen so many of these projects, Ms. Biederman, that I have to say congratulations for coming up with it! And fish? Perfect for Big Lake! That's important, don't you think? Like cows were just right for Chicago, with the meatpacking industry and all."

Jazz didn't know where Storm was going with this. Why was she flattering the teacher, unless ...

"It would be such an honor," Storm continued, "to be part of this project and have the chance to raise money for the town. But I should shut up. I'm the newest student in your class, and I have no right to give input on a city project."

"Don't be silly, Storm!" Ms. B said. "I think it's wonderful that you're taking such an interest in our project."

"Really? You mean someone could get a fish, even though she hasn't lived here her whole life and only wants to contribute what she can?"

"Of course!" Ms. B exclaimed. "In fact, I think you're the perfect person to be in charge of one of the fish."

"You do?"

"I do."

Storm clasped her hands together like a grateful child. It was enough to make Jazz want to bolt from the room. "Ms. B, are you really trusting me to do whatever is best for this fish? I'm in charge of getting it decorated?"

"Absolutely," she said.

Gracie hopped out of her seat and dashed to the front to give Storm a high-five. She looked as happy as if she'd won it herself. "Way to go, Storm! You rock!"

Jazz didn't wait for the bell. She was out of her seat and to the door in seconds. Didn't they know how much she needed this? Gracie had seemed to understand. But she sure didn't get it now. So much for Grace Doe's powers of observation.

6

The rest of the morning Jazz worked hard to avoid bumping into Gracie and Storm. She was so focused on looking out for them in the cafeteria that she didn't even see Paul until he sat down across from her at the lunch table.

"Tough break in art class," Paul said. But he couldn't keep his lips from twitching. "The other choice, Storm, was a surprise. I thought maybe Brittany or even Manny."

"At least Storm has an imagination," Jazz muttered.

Brittany and Manny were two more "copy artists." Neither one of them really liked art that much. Jazz kept these thoughts to herself and opened her box of Animal Crackers. She'd planned to buy lunch, but she didn't want to run into Storm in the food line, so she was stuck with what she had in her pack.

"You're eating cookies for lunch?" Paul asked, sneering at them, while he spread out his carefully packed lunch of yogurt, fruit, raisins, celery sticks, a tuna sandwich, and a juice box.

"Crackers," she corrected, although Animal Crackers technically had to be cookies.

"It's a big responsibility representing our school in the public art project." Paul opened the yogurt and sprinkled in his box of raisins. "I'm trying to decide between a bass and a perch. Both would be part of the Big Lake population, if we had a real lake."

"How logical of you," Jazz said, biting off the head of an elephant. "Say, if I find a fish in here, I'll give it to you for a model."

"Animal Crackers!" Storm plopped herself next to Paul and put one arm around his shoulder. "Man, don't you wish we had some, Paul? Did you know that Animal Crackers were introduced for Christmas, 1902? And the box had a string so you could hang it from your Christmas tree." She reached across the table and dug into Jazz's box until she found a bear, which she promptly popped into her mouth after removing her wad of gum.

Paul scooted a few inches away from Storm. "I suppose mutual congratulations are in order, Storm. Have you decided on the type of fish you'll portray?"

Jazz pretended not to listen.

"Me?" Storm laughed.

"Yes, you." Paul sounded confused.

"Are you kidding? *Me* paint a fish? Mestizos eat fish. We don't paint them."

"But you said — " Paul started.

"I said that I'd love to be in charge of decorating the fish. Weren't you listening? I specifically asked Ms. B if she'd trust me to do what was best for that fish."

"So?"

"So, what's best for that fish definitely isn't me. I'd get bored before I finished painting a fin." Storm reached over and took a handful of Jazz's Animal Crackers. "I think we all know what would be best for that fish, don't you, Paul? Jasmine Fletcher."

Jazz looked up at Storm.

Storm grinned. "Right, Jazz?"

Paul slammed down his celery stalk. "You can't do that! That's ... that's cheating!"

"Excuse me?" Storm said. "Ms. B and I have it all worked out." She turned to Jazz. "You're in, girlfriend. *You* are painting my fish."

"But ..." Jazz didn't know if Storm was kidding or not. "But she wanted *you* to do it, Storm. I'm the last person Ms. B wants to have a fish."

"Don't be whack. She knows you've got more talent than any of us. She just thinks you're a little 'out there.' So she solemnly charged me to be a responsible supervisor for my fish. But the job's yours."

Paul threw what was left of his lunch into his sack and stormed away from the table.

"Was it something I said?" Storm asked.

"How about *everything* you said?" Jazz suggested.

Storm took the last cookie. "Am I good, or what?"

"Good? You're great!"

Gracie slipped into Paul's vacated seat. "Guess you told her, huh?"

"You knew?" Jazz asked.

Gracie raised her eyebrows. "Only from the second Storm started spouting fish facts. Didn't you see her making faces at us during class?"

Jazz had seen it, but she hadn't read it. Not like Gracie.

Storm sighed. "Gracie started it. She kept pointing to you, then to Ms. B and making this mad-angry face until I figured out she was trying to tell me that you were making our teacher so angry she'd never give you one of those fish. So I decided I'd get one for you."

"Were we in the same class?" Jazz hadn't picked up on any of the signs. "Thanks, guys. I still can't believe you worked it out with Ms. B.

What did you say to her?"

"I waited until everyone left," Storm began.

"Except me," Gracie interrupted. "I'm invisible though."

"And?" Jazz wished she could have been there.

"Your basic fish talk," Storm explained. "I told her about 'spat,' which is what you call a baby oyster, and the 'elver,' which, of course, is a baby eel. Then we moved on to shrimp because I admire them for always and only swimming backward, not to mention the fact that a shrimp's heart is in his brain."

Annie Lind stopped behind Storm and waved her cheerleading friends on. "Did you just say something about a heart in a brain? Now there's a column for Professor Love."

"Go on, Storm!" Jazz demanded.

"So that's when I promised her that I would do whatever was best for that fish, even if it meant getting someone who was better than me to paint it."

"Ms. B didn't even hesitate," Gracie added. "She said she totally trusted Storm's judgment."

"But what did she say when you told her you wanted me to paint it?" Jazz asked.

"She said she knew you could do a great job all right," Storm said.

"But . . . ?" Jazz knew there was a "but" to this story.

Storm seemed to be choosing her words. "Well, she did have a few concerns about your tendencies toward the abstract."

"She called it 'the absurd,'" Gracie confided. "But she did say the part about you having talent."

It was more than Jazz would have expected.

Storm nodded. "And the bottom line is, you're in! You and Paul have to turn your designs in by tomorrow. You should stop by the art room and get the canvas or paper or whatever. And you have to choose which fiberglass fish you'll work on, although they're all the same. I guess there are twelve of them in store windows. So you just pick where you want to work."

"Ooh! Choose the one at Mom's!" Annie cried.

Jazz, and everybody else, stared up at Annie. "Your mom has one of the fish?"

"I guess. It came yesterday after I'd asked Mom about letting you put a mural on another wall. And by the way, she would love that, but she said she doesn't have another wall for a mural, which I guess is true now that I think about it."

"Annie!" Gracie interrupted. "The fish? Why didn't you tell us about it?"

"I didn't know it was for art. I thought it was supposed to go with the beach stuff Mom gets for the shop. Sorry. But wouldn't it be cool if you got to paint that one? Mom would love it!"

"That'd be great, Annie," Jazz agreed. "This could be the perfect solution for me, too."

"And that business proposition?" Storm asked.

Jazz nodded. She wished she hadn't gone off on Gracie earlier. Gracie had been right to tell the others about it. "Thanks. All of you."

They walked out of the cafeteria together.

"So what kind of fish are you going to paint?" Storm asked.

Without even thinking about it, a dozen ideas popped into Jazz's mind. The "Big Lake" didn't exist, except in the minds of its residents. So the fish was a fish out of water. Was it dreaming of the lake? Or was there a lake nobody but the fish could see? Jazz could visualize a narrative painting, a story in lines and colors and —

But she had to push those thoughts out of her head. "I guess I better go to the library and see what fish are in Ohio lakes," she said.

"That sounds exciting," Gracie commented sarcastically.

Jazz agreed with the sarcasm, but none of that mattered. If traditional was what would sell, what would get her what she wanted, then traditional was what they'd get.

7

As soon as school was out, Jazz dropped by the art room. "I just wanted to thank you for giving me a chance to participate in the public art project, Ms. Biederman. I promise not to let you down."

Ms. B twitched a smile that disappeared. "Jazz, I'm sure you can do an excellent job."

"Thanks. Would it be okay if I worked on the fish at Sam's Sammich Shop?"

Ms. B smiled. "Certainly. I'll mark that down."

"What about me?" Paul scurried into the room. He was carrying a stack of books, and his pack looked loaded, too. "Where's *my* fish?"

Ms. B read him a list of businesses that were hosting the contest.

"She's already got the best location," Paul whined. "Main and Claremont? I guess I'll have to take the other one on Main, Crafts-R-Us."

Jazz fought down a laugh. Paul would get constant advice from the owner of that shop. Mrs. Pulaski was so nice that Jazz had stopped going in there. The woman had followed her around, trying to talk her out of every decision — different beads, better thread, brighter colors.

Ms. B gave them each a canvas bag filled with supplies. "You'll find a special tracing canvas rolled up in there. Take good care of it. It's been outlined with the exact specifications of the fiberglass fish. Do your designs right on the canvas. Then all you'll have to do is trace your design onto the fish and paint. I see no problem with you completing the work before Saturday, do you?"

"No, ma'am," Paul answered.

Jazz couldn't believe they wouldn't give them more time. On the other hand, how much time did it take to paint a fish so it looked like a fish?

Ms. B continued, "The judges will visit each project Saturday morning and announce their decisions by noon. The silent auction begins Saturday morning at seven a.m. and ends sometime that afternoon. Then we'll be seeing fish all over Big Lake!"

Jazz couldn't wait to see what was in the sack of supplies. She felt through her bag. There were new brushes and a dozen tubes of paint. "Acrylics?" she asked.

"You have a problem with acrylics?" Ms. B sounded as if she'd been expecting Jazz to complain.

"No!" Jazz liked acrylics. "Coated acrylics are great, especially since some of the statues will end up outside, right?" Actually, she would have preferred to use sign enamels or automotive paints. She'd read about actual marine materials, gel coats, that could be top coated with Imron for a high gloss. If she'd really gotten to choose, though, she might have tried other materials, like faux stone finishes, so the finished fish would look dirtier and get more character the older it got. Or powdered metals that would look like bronze.

"Some of the statues will be outside, and some might be in business lobbies," Ms. B explained. "Everyone gets to work on his or her fish inside, however. We all know how fickle Ohio weather can be. The stores will set up the fish in front windows, where everyone can watch."

Jazz thought that was a terrible idea, but she didn't say so.

Paul frowned over at Jazz while he said to Ms. B, "Just make sure she understands that we don't want anything … anything …"

"Creative?" Jazz supplied.

"Perhaps the word Paul was searching for was 'controversial.'" Ms. B glanced from one to the other. "Don't forget. I need those sketches by class time tomorrow."

As soon as she got home, Jazz ran straight to her room and pulled out the fish canvas. It was thin, almost transparent, stretching a little over four feet wide. She weighted it down with her shoes on each end and got out her own sketching pencil. The fish stared up at her, a black outline, traced on the canvas and waiting to be traced onto a fiberglass fish. It felt weird to know that eleven other people were working with the exact same image.

Jazz got her pack and retrieved the fish book she'd checked out of the library. The whole fish section on the nature shelves had been ripped off by Paul, which explained his stack of books in the art room. Jazz was pretty sure she had all she needed, though. She'd found a picture of a largemouth bass and hadn't been able to get it out of her head. It was as if the fish were crying or screaming. The picture was so firmly in her mind, including the shades of green and the pinkish speckled highlights, that she wouldn't have needed to bring the book home with her.

But she wanted to get it right. So she opened to the page she'd marked, and she began sketching onto the canvas, making sure the shape of each scale was just right. In spite of her focus, her resolve to reproduce that fish exactly, she couldn't stop her mind from flashing images of the fish's tail sweeping through the air. Her imagination was somewhere else, hearing sounds from this wide-open mouth, a cry for help or a cry of praise?

She heard a noise and turned to see Ty and Kendra standing behind her. "You scared me, guys."

"Sorry," Ty said. "Why are you drawing a fish?"

"Kind of a long story," Jazz said. "But with any luck, this fish will be my ticket to having my own art studio right here in the house."

"You can make money drawing fish?" Ty asked, frowning down on the outline.

"That's the plan." Jazz smiled at Kendra, who was holding one of her trademark stick-figure drawings. "Nice picture, Kendra," she said. "For me?"

Kendra shook her head.

"Ah. Who's it for?" Jazz asked.

"For my brother," she answered.

Jazz grinned at Ty. "Well, lucky you, Ty."

Ty didn't grin back. "It's not for me."

"I don't get it," Jazz said.

"It's for DC," Ty said, looking sheepish.

Jazz's throat went dry, and she had to swallow. Why would Kendra draw a picture for a brother who had died before she was born?

Ty twisted his baseball cap in his hands. "Kind of my fault. I was helping Kendra with her homework assignment."

"We draw *all* our family," Kendra chimed in.

Jazz remembered when she'd had the same assignment in elementary school. She'd hated it. She'd tried to get her parents to tell her when DC's birthday was, what his favorite color was, what he'd wanted to be when he grew up. Neither one of them would talk about her brother, and she'd ended up erasing him from her family tree. "You didn't do anything wrong, Ty. Kendra should know about her brother." She reached up and pulled Kendra into a hug.

Kendra dropped to her knees and hugged Jazz back. "I miss my brother," she said.

"Sweetie," Jazz said, smoothing Kendra's hair, "you never got to meet DC. Are you sure you miss him?"

Kendra's head nodded several times. "I miss him more. I never got to see him."

Jazz didn't know what to say. She rubbed her cheek on top of Kendra's head. Her hair smelled like strawberries. "I know." Jazz understood. "You do miss him." It was amazing to Jazz. Her sister, who had trouble adding seven and three, was deep enough to miss someone she'd never seen. Kendra's big brother was real to her. So what if she'd never seen him? DC was real. And Kendra knew it. "You really are an artist, Kendra. You know that?"

The door pushed the rest of the way open, and their mother stood on the other side. "I was wondering where everybody had disappeared to. Why aren't you outside enjoying the nice weather? I hear it's turning on us tomorrow."

Jazz rolled up her canvas as fast as she could.

"Jasmine?" Mom asked, her voice tight, suspicious. "What are you doing there? Is that another art project?" She stepped closer.

"It's a fish!" Kendra exclaimed.

"A fish?" Mom turned to Ty. "Ty, will you and Kendra go set the table for dinner, please?"

Jazz braced herself for another fight. "I'm sorry, Mom. I didn't know I couldn't even draw in my room. I thought you just meant — "

"Is that fish for the public art project?" Mom interrupted. "The Mayor's 'Go Fish' campaign? Those fiberglass monstrosities he plans to put up all over the city?"

It didn't take Gracie's powers of deduction for Jazz to figure out that Mom hated this project. "How do you know about it?" she asked.

"I'm on the City Planning Commission, Jasmine. You know that. And I was the only one who voted against this crazy fish idea. Honestly, they said things like, 'This will make a big *splash* in our city,' and 'Let's make it *o-fish-al*,' and 'Now we have to go *fishing* for sponsors — *reel* soon.' Then they laughed as if they were the funniest people on the planet."

Jazz knew her mother was on every major committee going. She just never imagined Mom would have anything to do with art. "I thought the whole fish thing was pretty lame, too. But I guess these public art projects pay off."

"Mmmm."

"Our art teacher got to give two students in our art class a chance to decorate one of the fish. So … I ended up being one of them."

"Really?"

Jazz wanted her mother to know that the project would make money, that *her* fish could be sold for real money. "They auction off the fish when we're all done."

"I know," Mom said.

"So...." Jazz wasn't sure how to drive the point home. "*My* fish, my art project, could make money."

Slowly, her mother seemed to let that sink in. She nodded. "The business proposition. Hmmm." Jazz couldn't read Mom's expression. Then she pivoted and walked to the door. "Dinner in ten minutes, Jasmine." And she was gone.

8

Dinner was quiet. Ty tried to get a conversation going by talking about his and Mick's baseball schedule. Jazz just wanted to finish and get back to her fish.

Then Kendra dropped the bomb. "Did DC like cooked carrots?" She was holding one in her fingers and studying it, as if words were written on the limp orange vegetable.

Ty flinched, then looked to Jazz for help.

Before Jazz could explain, Dad answered firmly, "I don't know. And it doesn't matter." He said it without looking up from his baked chicken.

But Kendra wasn't finished. "I don't like them. I wonder if DC liked them. Maybe because they're pretty. And orange."

Jazz didn't know what to say. To Kendra or to Dad.

Dad plunked his fork down harder than he needed to. "Kendra?"

Mom looked up from her plate and stared at the unlit candle in the pewter candlestick holder. It sat in the exact center of the lace tablecloth. "No, Kendra. DC didn't like cooked carrots either."

It was the most Jazz could remember Mom talking about her oldest son.

Kendra's smile grew huge. "Yes!" she exclaimed, setting down her carrot and digging into the mashed potatoes.

The rest of the meal passed in silence, except for chewing noises. Jazz skipped dessert and tore upstairs to her room, where she worked on the fish until after midnight. When she was finished, she had a fish that would have fooled a school of bass.

Jazz didn't get much sleep the rest of the night. She knew she'd done her best at making her design look exactly like the picture of a largemouth bass. But what if the picture hadn't been accurate? Paul probably had a dozen or more pictures he could work from, and she'd only used one measly photo. And what about that large mouth? She was thinking about using another medium for the big mouth, but maybe that would kill her chances in the contest.

Then her mind flip-flopped to the invisible fish in the invisible lake. Half-asleep, she could smell lake and fish and see the way the bass surfaced and shouted to the other fish that it was real and it could fly. Kendra was there, and so was DC, smiling, riding that fish like he knew so much more than anybody stuck on earth. And Jazz was there, seeing it all, wishing she could capture it on canvas.

Tuesday morning Jazz caught a ride to school with her dad. The sky threatened rain. Usually, Jazz would have welcomed a walk in the autumn rain. She loved the way it smelled, like an electrical promise. She loved the things the wind did before a storm — making leaves dance and branches sway, performing invisible tricks on everything under the sky. But today she had to worry about getting her fish design to art class.

Dad pulled up to the curb, and Storm Novelo came trotting down the sidewalk to meet them. She was wearing a white silk jogging suit with high-heeled sandals. She'd pulled back her hair into a ponytail, and it looked cool. Jazz ran her fingers through her thick, wavy hair and wished she'd taken a bit more time with it in front of the mirror.

"Thanks for the lift, Dad," she said, gathering her pack and canvas and checking the backseat. "Tell Mom not to wait on me for dinner. I've got to work on the fish. I'll be at Sam's Sammich Shop if you need me."

Dad frowned, and Jazz could see he had no idea what she was talking about.

"Public art contest? Mom can fill you in."

"All right. But homework first."

"Nice ride!" Storm exclaimed as Jazz slid out and shut the car door.

"Thank you," Dad answered.

Jazz and Storm walked into school together. "So?" Storm tried to peer into the rolled-up canvas, but Jazz pulled it away. "Jazz, did you finish the design? Does it look like a fish, for real?"

"Let's hope so," Jazz said.

"We should be doing sea fish," Storm commented, as she followed Jazz to her locker and waited while Jazz put books in and pulled books out. "I read last night that only one in a thousand animals born in the sea lives to maturity! Ninety-nine percent of lobsters die a few weeks after hatching. Isn't that sad? And expensive! Odds are ten thousand to one against a lobster ever getting old enough to be eaten. And then if he *does* live that long, we have him for dinner! I'm never eating lobster again."

"I'm sure they appreciate that, Storm," Jazz muttered as they entered the art room.

Gracie had saved seats on the front row, which wasn't hard to do in art. In front of the room stood two big easels, and on one aluminum easel was a painting of a giant fish.

Paul sat next to Jazz on the front row. "What do you think?"

Jazz studied the drawing, which was exactly the same shape and size as hers. It was good, realistic, obviously a regular bass. He'd gotten the black spots in perfect alignment and the scales precisely placed. "It's great, Paul," she admitted.

"Did you get yours done?" he asked.

"I think so."

Ms. B walked to the first easel and pointed to Paul's fish. "Class, I want you to take a look at Paul's design for the 'Go Fish' campaign. Isn't it wonderful?" She clapped, and the class joined in. "You can watch Paul paint his design onto the fiberglass model fish in the window of Crafts-R-Us on Main Street all week."

"Looks good enough to eat!" someone yelled from the back.

Ms. B turned to Jazz. "Storm had some reservations about painting the fish herself, so we've designated Jasmine Fletcher as our second entry from this class."

Jazz waited for protests, but there weren't any. She figured she and Paul were the only students who cared enough about art to put in all this work with no grade benefit.

"Jasmine?" Ms. B was calling her. "Will you please put your design up here for us?"

Jazz didn't move.

"Go!" Storm shoved her out of the chair.

Jazz's hands shook as she unrolled the canvas. "Um ... it may change when I paint the fish. I can still do more to it." She clipped it to the easel and rushed back to her seat.

"Wow!" Storm exclaimed. "That's so fly!"

Around the room, Jazz could hear other kids: "Man!" "Cool!" "She's good!"

"Nice job, Jasmine!" Even Ms. B sounded pleased. "Colors are true. Very lifelike."

"What about the mouth?" Paul asked. "How's she going to finish off the mouth?"

Jazz rushed to her own defense. "I told you I still had work to do. It's a largemouth bass, and I thought I could build the large mouth with putty and automotive gloss." She could tell Ms. B wasn't crazy about the idea. "Or maybe a molding?" Still, her teacher frowned, head cocked to one side. "Or just paints? I could paint the inside of the mouth, like a real largemouth bass?"

Now Ms. B smiled again. "Yes. I think that would conform nicely."

Gracie leaned over to Jazz. "And that's what you want, right?"

It occurred to Jazz that Gracie was the only one who hadn't complimented her on the fish. "You don't like it."

Gracie breathed in, then let out all her air, like a pinpricked balloon. "It's a great fish, Jazz. It's just ... it's just not what I think of when I think about your art. God gave you an amazing talent. I'm just not sure you're using it."

God again? Jazz turned and studied her own fish. It *was* a great fish. Ms. B liked it. Even Paul looked worried, like he was actually facing the possibility of defeat. Gracie was just being Gracie.

Jazz may have been the only one studying in last-hour study hall, but she finished all her homework so she'd be able to start to work on the real fish. She and Annie met up after school and waited for Mick by the middle school. Then they hiked to Sam's Sammich Shop together.

"Storm said your fish blew Paul's away," Annie commented, as they dodged around a pack of slow-moving middle-school girls.

"Way to go, Jazz!" Mick said. She was wearing a Cleveland Indian's ball cap, and her ponytail swished as she walked backward in front of them.

"It's just a fish," Jazz replied, remembering the look on Gracie's face in class.

Mick stumbled, but kept walking backward. "Aaron Leigh, our second baseman, says his dad gets to paint one of the fish, the one in Burger King on Claremont. His dad's in commercial design and works for some company in Cleveland. But I'll bet his won't stand a chance against yours."

"Mom's psyched that you're painting the fish in the shop," Annie said. "She felt awful when she had to say no to another mural."

"Your mom's great." Jazz meant it. Except for once, when Samantha Lind had a date with Annie's English teacher, Jazz had never seen the two of them fight, not the way Jazz and her mom got into it anyway. "As long as she doesn't overdo the Beach Boys music while I'm there. It took me a year to get those songs out of my head."

In the front picture window of the shop stood a white fish on a pedestal. It looked bigger than Jazz had imagined it. "Are you sure your mom didn't get Moby Dick by mistake?"

she asked, staring through the "Sam's Sammich Shop" letters
painted on the glass. Doubts multiplied as she stood there.
Her fear kept growing until it was as big as the stupid-
looking fish. What made her think she could paint something
that would win the contest, or something that anybody else in
Big Lake would actually pay money for?

In her mind Jazz pictured the white fish flying, soaring
through the glass and into the air, free. There was a story
here. That's how she felt about her art — like the picture, the
image, already existed somewhere, and it was her job, her
privilege, to unravel it.

Only not this time.

9

Annie, Mick, and Jazz sat at the table nearest the front window, where they had the best view of the fish. Samantha Lind had given up her prime window table for the fish. Customers fought for that spot.

"I was hoping you'd come by." Annie's mom smiled down at them. She looked more like Annie's sister than her mother, with the same auburn hair and perfect face. Jazz would have liked to do a charcoal of Samantha Lind. Her eyes said she'd lived through a lot and come out stronger. She'd been doing the single-mom thing Annie's whole life. "Lemonade on the house."

They thanked her. And when she came back, she set down three lemonades and three Ice Creams à la Mick.

Jazz couldn't finish her ice cream. She was too anxious to get started on the fish project. She pushed herself from the table. "Well, no sense putting this off any longer." She walked to the fish, but she wasn't sure where to start. She wondered if this was what it felt like to go fishing, trying to figure out which lure might work.

The light was great. With her back to the window, Jazz got out her design. She had read about contemporary artists, like

John Clem Clarke, who used a mylar maquette, kind of like
the transparent cels cartoonists used. They did a preliminary
drawing and then used the cel as an overlay for the canvas.
That's what she was supposed to do with her design. She took
it out and unrolled it. When she placed it on the fiberglass
fish, the translucent canvas stuck. It was a perfect fit. Now all
she had to do was trace her design onto both sides of the fish
and paint.

It felt more like drafting than drawing as she carefully
traced over the lines and designs. She couldn't shake the
feeling that this was cheating. But it wasn't. She'd done the
design. Still, it almost didn't feel like hers. There was no
surprise, no discovery.

She'd finished with one side of the fish and had moved
to the other side, when she heard Gracie's voice: "Hey, Fish
Woman, how's it going?"

Storm was right behind Gracie. She'd forgotten to take
off her "Hi! I'm Storm!" name tag from the supermarket. Or
maybe she was wearing it as part of her outfit, which kind
of screamed the same thing. Storm Novelo was wearing red,
totally. From head to toe, shoes to beret, and everything in
between. "Your supervisor is here, Jazz! Is it fish yet?"

The shop had filled with high school kids while Jazz had
been tracing. Annie was sitting with a couple of football guys,
and Mick was helping Sam take orders.

Gracie examined the fiberglass fish. "You're going to be
done with this way before Saturday at this rate."

By six o'clock, Jazz had traced her design onto the fish,
and it looked as if Gracie had been right. Jazz figured
another day to paint ought to do it.

Jazz was wrong. By six o'clock the next day, she'd barely completed the undercoating. The problem was that she couldn't stay focused. Every time someone walked by, she looked up. She eavesdropped on conversations going around the shop. And she took breaks, way too many breaks.

"You're bored," Gracie said. She'd stopped by the shop and stayed for dinner.

Jazz had taken advantage of the opportunity to stop working and joined Gracie for a cheeseburger. "But I'm *never* bored when I'm painting or sculpting. I just can't work here. There are too many distractions."

Gracie shook her head. "I've seen you get so lost in a painting in art class that you didn't even know a fist fight was going on in the room. I've seen Ms. B have to kick you out of the art room because the next class was already there and you didn't even notice."

Jazz had to admit Gracie had a point. She did lose herself in her art, and it didn't matter what else was going on around her. "Well, if I don't get down to business soon, I'm not going to get this thing finished."

"Wow," Gracie said sarcastically. "Then there'd only be eleven big fish in Big Lake. I better leave and let you get on with it."

But Jazz didn't get on with it. She left early, without even breaking open her acrylics.

Thursday Jazz walked to school. It had rained most of the night, and the sky promised more. Jazz took her time, tiptoeing around some puddles and splashing through others. Today she just didn't care about anything. Not about the fish. Not about the art project. In her head, she'd still do anything to win the business deal with her mom and to get her own art studio. But her heart just wasn't in it.

She knew when she walked up the sidewalk to Big Lake High that the bell had already rung. Except for one student who hopped out of her car and ran in from the parking lot, the grounds were empty.

Jazz poked along the deserted hall to art class, without checking in at the office for a late slip. She was just too tired to jump through school hoops today.

"Where've you been?" Storm met her at the door and pulled her into the closest seat. Ms. B was erasing something from the board and had her back to the class, which meant nobody was paying attention to anything. "Are you sick or something? Your shoes are wet, Jazz!"

Jazz shrugged. Her mother had bought the shoes, and she'd probably spent a fortune on them. Jazz wasn't that crazy about the brown leather Prada flats, but they'd kept her feet dry.

Paul proudly announced to the class that his fish was finished. "Most of the other artists, from what I've been able to see, are almost done with their projects, as well. But I do believe I'm the first to be completely finished. I hope you'll all stop by and take a look at my fish."

"That's wonderful news, Paul," Ms. B said. She looked around the room until her gaze fell on Jazz. "Jasmine, would you give us a progress report, please?"

Storm answered for her. "Right on schedule here! Should be done by tomorrow morning." As soon as Ms. B went back to her art lecture, Storm whispered to Jazz, "Your locker. Right after school."

But when school got out, Jazz couldn't bear to think of facing the big white fish. She skipped her locker and, instead, crossed town to Brookside Park, where she could be alone. Trees had started shedding, and a wet blanket of brown and burgundy covered the soft park lawn. The leaves swish-crunched as she walked on to the old band shell, a brick platform backed by a dome that looked like half an igloo. Open bleachers flanked the stage, the aisles like spokes rising away from the band shell.

Jazz strolled to the center of the benches and sat down after swiping it with her jacket sleeve. She was an audience of one. Here, she felt like an artist. Her mind pieced together honking geese overhead, the rustle of leaves, a woodpecker, shadows of branches on brick, and the smell of rain stuck in the clouds. She longed to paint what she could feel, what she could see in her head. There was so much beauty here.

Jazz sat there until the faint sun set behind the band shell in a bank of gray clouds. She shivered from the damp bench and cool breeze that had blown in. A rumble of thunder woke her from her daydream, and she started the long walk home.

The first raindrop hit as Jazz reached her front door. She slipped inside, shut the door, then heard the crash of thunder. Instantly, rain pelted the roof. Another blast of thunder shook the windows.

Kendra ran up to Jazz and gave her a bear hug.

"You're home rather early." Mom joined them. She put one hand on Kendra's hair. "You're not scared of the thunder, are you, honey? I thought you liked thunder."

Kendra smiled up as she released Jazz from her hug. "I love thunder!" She smiled over at the stairs, and Jazz saw Ty sitting there. "Ty says God is bowling, but it's only a joke. I don't think God has time to bowl, do you?"

She'd addressed her question to her mother, who seemed to struggle with an answer.

Finally, Ty spoke up. "Kendra, you know I was kidding about God bowling, right?"

Another crash of thunder shook the house.

"God isn't too busy to watch me play puzzles, right? Or help me with my work from school?"

"Nah." Ty stood up and walked down to the landing. "You ought to come to church with me, Kendra. Mick keeps asking if you will." Mick and Gracie and Annie had probably asked Jazz a hundred times if she'd go with them. And she'd turned them down a hundred times.

Kendra swung around to face her mom. "Can I? Can I go with Ty and Mick?"

Jazz was rooting for a yes answer — not because it would do her sister any good, but because Kendra wanted it so much.

"Please, Mommy?"

Even Jazz's mom couldn't say no to that face. "I suppose."

Kendra ran up to Ty. "Call Mick, Ty! Let's go."

"Not until Sunday. This is only Thursday, kid. You can call Mick and tell her the news if you want to."

Kendra raced off toward the kitchen.

Jazz started upstairs, but her mom stopped her.

"Jasmine, I happened to walk by that sandwich shop this afternoon. Don't you have to finish your project before Saturday?"

"It's not going to take me very long to paint it," Jazz said, her chest tightening at the mention of the big white fish.

Mom nodded. "Ah. I suppose not." She walked off, leaving Ty and Jazz alone in the front room.

"Jazz?" Ty had just started calling her "Jazz," like her friends did.

"Hmm?"

"Is it because of DC and all?"

Jazz frowned at her little brother. "Is what because of DC?"

"Is that why we never go to church together?"

"I don't know, Ty. Probably."

"Is that why *you* don't want to go?" he asked, following her up the stairs when she tried to walk past him.

"Yeah. I guess. I just don't think there's anybody out there, Ty. He wasn't there when our brother got shot. That's for sure."

"Mick says in heaven things like shootings don't happen. But earth's not heaven, and bad stuff happens."

Jazz could tell Ty wanted to talk more, but she didn't. "I've got work, Ty." She took the steps two at a time.

Inside her room she plopped on her bed and shut her eyes. She tried as hard as she could to remember DC, to latch on to anything she could recall about him. But she'd been too young. Her parents didn't have DC's picture on the "family picture" wall in the family room. But she'd seen pictures of DC, buried as deeply in her parents' closet as her art projects had been buried in hers. DC had looked a lot like Ty.

She'd just gotten to sleep when her cell went off. She reached it just before it switched over to voice mail. "What?"

"Jazz?" It was Storm's voice, but she heard others in the background — Annie's, Mick's, and at least a couple of guys. Jazz suspected Storm was calling from Sam's.

"Jasmine Fletcher," Storm commanded, "this is your supervisor speaking, and I will accept no excuses. We'll be at your house in ten minutes. You will report for fish duty."

10

Jazz rode in the back with Storm, and Mick took the passenger front while Annie drove them in a chilly drizzle to Sam's Sammich Shop.

Jazz didn't speak until they were almost there. "Okay. Whose big idea was this?"

Nobody took credit.

"I said I'd finish the stupid fish, and I'll finish it," Jazz insisted.

"We know you will," Storm said. Her yellow plastic raincoat and yellow boots made her look like the Morton Salt girl. "Now."

Annie parked as close as she could get to the shop, which seemed to mean one wheel up on the curb, and they all dashed inside.

Sam met them at the door. "Good evening, one and all. Jazz, your fans, my customers, have been asking about you all day."

Annie threw her coat over the already-full hall tree. "Well, you can tell the customers that the show is about to begin."

"And end!" Storm exclaimed. She turned to Jazz, and Jazz had never seen such a look of determination on Storm's face.

"You're not leaving here until that fish is finished. Painted. Done."

"But — " Jazz began.

"Because," Storm continued, "*we're* not leaving until that fish is done."

Storm wasn't kidding. She and Annie and Mick closed in around Jazz as she faced off with the big white fish. They watched as she got out her acrylics and mixed her colors.

Jazz had no trouble creating the right shade of green or washing the underbelly with just the right touch of pink. The paints dried fast, so she found that by the time she finished the fish belly, she could work the stripes onto the back without the colors running.

Every time she got bored, which was every five minutes, she begged for a break. But her captors refused. They took shifts standing guard while she worked on the spots on the fish's back. Whenever she slowed down, they had their ways of keeping her going. Storm snap-popped her gum with a vengeance. Annie signaled for her mom to crank up the Beach Boys. Mick started explaining the intricacies of the infield fly and double plays, which turned out to be more boring than fish.

"You're bored, aren't you, Jazz?" Mick said.

Jazz stopped staring out the window and picked up her paintbrush again. "No, I'm not, Mick. Tell me about that fly rule again."

Mick laughed. "I didn't mean bored with baseball. How could anybody get bored with baseball? I meant with the fish. Gracie said you weren't finishing it because you were bored with it."

As soon as Mick said it, Jazz knew it was the truth. But it didn't make it sting any less. "Well, Gracie doesn't always know everything about everything." Jazz got down on her knees and painted faster, working the specks between the lines of green and brown.

By closing time, Jazz had the fish all finished, except for the mouth.

Sam brought out grilled cheese and milkshakes to celebrate. "I have to admit," she confided, "I never thought you could finish it tonight."

"They didn't leave me much choice," Jazz complained. But she grinned at her friends and hoped they knew how much she appreciated their bossy interference. She couldn't honestly say that she'd enjoyed painting that fish, but she was really going to enjoy having it finished.

"So where's Gracie?" Sam asked.

Mick started to answer. "She's working on her bl — "

Jazz saw Storm kick Mick under the table. It was a miracle that Mick had kept Gracie's blogging a secret for so many months.

"They give us so much homework," Storm said, smiling at Mick, who was rubbing her shin, but looking grateful for the kick.

"I'll stay and close up if you want to get home, Mom," Annie offered. "Did Gramps go home?"

Jazz had seen Annie's grandparents at the shop a lot. Her grandfather cooked, and her grandmother played waitress.

"He went home half an hour ago," Sam answered. "Are you serious about closing? And cleaning the kitchen?"

"I'll stay and help," Mick answered.

"That would be great, guys." Sam rubbed that same place between her neck and her shoulder that always bothered Jazz after she'd gotten lost in her art and stayed hunched over a canvas or a sculpture for too many hours. "It's stopped raining, at least for now. I'll walk home, and you can give the girls a ride if they need it. Deal?"

"Deal," Annie answered.

Storm, Annie, and Mick swept and cleaned the shop, while Jazz worked on the largemouth's large mouth. She couldn't help imagining that mouth open for a purpose, poised on the verge of a great exclamation, some truth it had to shout to the world. She thought of a dozen ways she could mold the mouth and give it dimension, and another dozen ways she could do even more with abstract and nothing but paints.

But she didn't go there. She just painted the mouth to look like the bass in her picture.

As Mick and Annie double-checked the kitchen to make sure nothing was left on, Jazz put the last line around the fish's gills.

"Done!" she yelled.

Storm leaped into a victory dance, and Jazz packed up her paints and stashed them in the supply closet. "I'll leave these here one more night, okay, Annie? All that's left is the legend. I can write that tomorrow after school. Then I'm done. Finished. Free!"

"What's a legend?" Mick asked. "I mean, I know what a legend is, like a myth or something? Do you have to write one about your fish?"

"Wouldn't that be tight?" Storm said. "Like make up a story for each fish!"

"Not exactly." Jazz put on her jacket. "We're supposed to write something about our fish and why we painted them like we did. Something like that." She yawned. Right now she couldn't think of a single word to write. Where was Miss Big-Shot-Writer Grace Doe when you needed her? It didn't matter though. She could whip off the legend after school tomorrow and be done with the whole thing. Then all she'd have to do is wait and ... Jazz almost told herself "wait and *pray*." It was weird how that word popped into her head, when she didn't believe in prayer. You couldn't believe in prayer when you didn't believe in God. Of course she couldn't pray. She'd just have to wait and *hope* her fish would win.

It wasn't that late when Jazz got home, but the house was quiet. She found Mom in her office on the phone, so they just waved good night to each other. Dad wasn't home. Spiels had executive meetings on lots of Thursday nights, and Jazz figured that's where Dad was. Ty was in his room, half-asleep over his math book.

She peeked in on Kendra, thinking she'd already be asleep.

"Jasmine!" Kendra cried. She sat up in bed and held out her arms. The bedside light was on, and crayons and notebook paper were strewn all over the bed.

"Are you drawing in bed again?" Jazz asked, hugging her sister, then picking up paper after paper, all with Kendra's trademark stick person drawn on them. The drawings were so much alike that they could have come from a copy machine. "Who are all these for?"

Kendra crossed her arms at her chest. "I made them for DC, but I don't know where to put them."

Jazz wasn't sure what to say. Most of the time she felt she understood her sister pretty well and knew what Kendra could grasp and what she couldn't. "You know he's dead, right, honey?"

Kendra grinned. "Yes, silly! He's in heaven with Jesus. Ty said so."

Jazz was glad Ty had played the "heaven" card, not that he didn't believe it himself. She was sure he did. The thought of DC in heaven had made Kendra so happy, so peaceful, that for a minute Jazz wished she could believe it herself.

"How about if I take care of DC's pictures for you, Kendra?" Jazz tucked the drawings into her pack and kissed her sister good night. Then she went straight to the bathroom and took a long, hot bath.

Under a cloud of bubbles, Jazz relaxed and let her mind go wherever it wanted to. She closed her eyes and imagined flying fish, their mouths filled with golden words, soaring through wavy streaks and swirls of air that only the fish could see. It was the first time in a whole week that Jazz felt like an artist.

11

Jazz knew she should have felt great as she sat in her art class Friday morning. Ms. B had driven by Sam's Sammich Shop on her way to school, and she'd loved what she'd seen in the window. She'd been raving about Jazz's work for five minutes straight while poor Paul fumed.

"I want everybody in this classroom to check out Jasmine's fish in the window of Sam's Sammich Shop tomorrow morning, if not this afternoon. And Paul's, too, and all the other contestants' fish. I have a feeling our school may be bringing home the honors."

"Is there a trophy for the winner?" Storm asked. She was dressed as if the top half of her body had forgotten to consult the bottom half. The casual, worn-out, faded blue jeans and tennis shoes were topped with a gold silk blouse and mountains of gold jewelry — bracelets, necklaces, earrings, and barrettes.

"Well, not this year, Storm." Ms. B couldn't seem to stop smiling. "But they can feel good about raising money for Big Lake at the silent auction. People will be placing bids on Saturday. It's going to be so exciting!"

After school, Jazz walked by herself to the shop. Gracie had called a meeting at the cottage since they'd be tied up on Saturday with the art project and the judging. Jazz had promised to meet them after she had a chance to write up her legend for the fish.

Only as she crossed through Big Lake University's campus and cut back to downtown, she still couldn't come up with anything to write. Why *had* she painted her bass like she had? Because she wanted to win. Because her art teacher made it clear that this was the way everybody else was painting theirs. Jazz had a feeling these weren't the answers the city was looking for.

Instead of going in, Jazz stopped in front of the shop and stared in at her fish. The artists' kits had included a white erase board and marker, with instructions for writing the legend. Jazz's white display board rested on the pedestal below her fish. So far, all it had written on it was: LARGEMOUTH BASS BY JASMINE FLETCHER.

Finally, Jazz trudged inside and plopped down at the table next to her fish. She still couldn't think of one word to add to that legend.

Sam came and sat at the table with her. "Hi, Jazz. Annie said you guys were going to hang out at Gracie's cottage after school. What's up? I thought you were finished with your fish. It looks great, by the way. You should have seen poor Paul, that guy who painted the fish in the craft store window. When he saw your fish, that poor boy looked like he'd lost his best friend. Holden and I walked around last night and saw all the other fish. We both think yours is the best."

Holden was Holden Hamilton, the high school English teacher also known as "Hamlet" on the blog. Jazz knew he and Sam had chaperoned the homecoming dance as a date, and she'd seen them together a couple of times since then.

Annie and her mom must have come to an understanding about it, but it had to be weird for Annie. "Thanks," Jazz said. "I'm really glad it's over ... except for this legend thing I'm supposed to write."

"Well, I've gotten a lot of traffic by that window," Sam said. "I've heard so many good comments, your ears should have been on fire. Your mom seemed to like it a lot."

"My mom?"

"She's been by twice today. She didn't come in, but she stood outside the window and stared in at your fish for quite a while each time. Now your dad — "

"Dad was with her?" Jazz was amazed. As far as she knew, neither one of them came downtown in the middle of the day. She knew for a fact that Dad had lunch sent in at Spiels. And Mom was so picky with her diet that she packed her lunches.

"He wasn't with your mother," Sam explained. "He came just after the lunch crowd. I tried to talk him into Ice Cream à la Mick, but he didn't want anything except coffee."

"Dad came in? And drank coffee?"

"Three cups, which is really too much caffeine, especially if he drinks coffee for breakfast. He sat right here, where he had the best view of your fish." Sam got up when a group of high school kids burst in.

Jazz tried to imagine her dad here. He so didn't fit. She hated that all her parents had to see of her art was this plain largemouth bass. She wished they would have seen one of the pieces of art she was really proud of instead.

She tried to come up with a legend for the fish, but it was impossible to hear herself think over the obnoxious laughter of kids on all sides of her now. Jazz got up and walked out of the shop. They'd be waiting for her at the cottage. She could do the legend later.

By the time she got to the cottage, everybody else was already there.

Storm swiveled in the desk chair and announced, "Finished! Ahead of time, Ms. Doe, thank you very much!"

"Duly noted." Gracie motioned for Storm to vacate the computer, so she could sit there. "This, I gotta read."

. . . .
THAT'S WHAT YOU THINK!

DIDYANOSE

Looks can be deceiving. Life is filled with mystery! Did you know that things aren't always as they appear? Like. . .

- *It sure doesn't look like it, but your forearm (from inside your elbow to the inside of your wrist) is the same length as your foot.*
- *Your thigh bone is stronger than concrete.*
- *There are 12 (count them for yourself) flower designs on each Oreo.*
- *There's no banana in banana oil.*
- *Male mosquitoes aren't what you think they are. They're vegetarians! They feed on the nectar from flowers and don't bite humans. (Girl mosquitoes, on the other hand, drink blood and spread disease. But don't yell at them. Female mosquitoes are deaf!)*
- *Don't spiders look like they'd stick together? Not true. We all know the black widow loves to eat her dates. (And who*

can blame her?) But did you know that some species of baby spiders bite off the limbs of their mothers and slowly eat on them for weeks?

- *A crocodile gets 2000 – 3000 teeth over its lifetime and looks like he'd chew you up and spit you out if he could. Nope. They don't chew. They swallow food (and that includes other crocs on occasion) whole (a comforting thought).*
- *Science has so many mysteries that they have to make up theories to explain what they see . . . or don't see. Like Fritz Zwicky, who, in 1933, developed a theory that's still used by scientists to try to explain the universe and the gravitational forces we can't see. The "Theory of Dark Matter" says that some "unseen mass" must exist at the center of the galaxies, pulling them inward, because matter near the center moves faster. Curiouser and curiouser.*
- *Ever see a sunspot? Or energy? The energy released in one hour by just one little ol' sunspot would give us all the electrical power we'd need in the United States for the next million years. And what about wind? No, you haven't seen it. You've just seen what it does. Or time? Or — ?*

Gracie must have finished reading before Jazz did. "Solid," she said, scrolling down to where the "Professor Love" column should have been.

"Annie, what have you got for us?" Gracie demanded.

Annie sank into the big white chair and sighed. "Well, I did pick out which questions worked with the rest of the blog stuff, about people not being what they appear to be."

Mick came to her rescue. "And I typed them in. So all Annie has to do is answer the questions."

"I want to see them," Storm declared.

Everybody except Annie gathered around the screen to read the questions that had been sent in over the last week. There were only three posted, but Jazz knew there must be plenty more where those came from. Professor Love got more mail than the rest of them put together. Mick read the first question out loud, while Jazz read the screen herself.

. . . .
DEAR PROFESSOR LOVE

> *Dear Professor Love,*
>
> *How can this be? When I went out on my first date with TC, he was so sweet. He even opened the car door for me! He took me to the movie I wanted to see, and he paid 4 my popcorn! Now, one month later, I discover that he's a liar and a cheater! How could I have been so blind? I actually thought we would end up married, with 7 children (3 boys, 4 girls).*
>
> *— Signed, Temporarily blinded*

"So, Annie," Storm interrupted, "how are you going to answer this girl?"

"Oh, I don't know," Annie said slowly. "Nothing too encouraging. I'd never want these two to actually get together. I wouldn't do that to the gene pool. How about this?"

She spoke, and Mick typed:

> *Dear Temp,*
>
> *Even from here, I can see that you're leaving out big chunks of this story. Think about it. Replay what you*

*knew about this guy, what you'd heard about him, before
you went out that first time. Are you one of those girls
who can so often be heard saying, "I know he's awful, or
wild, or a player, with other girls, but he's different with
me"? That's called going in with your blinders firmly in
place. There's a lot more to a guy than what he can pull
off showing you for a few hours when he's on his best
behavior. Next time, because I have a feeling you're the
kind of female who has to have many "next times," keep
your eyes open. There's more to a guy than meets the
eye! (Consider the rhyme a bonus.)*

Love, Professor Love

Again, the "Professor Love" in Annie amazed Jazz. She'd
gone through a lot with guys herself. Maybe she'd learned
some of this stuff the hard way.

She read the next question:

Dear Professor Love,

*This girl (let's call her Mary) and I have been friends since
elementary school. I've always told her about other girls
I liked or went with. She's the one I'd go to for advice, to
give the female insights, you know? Now all of a sudden,
she's turned on me. One day, it was fine, like we'd always
been. You know, close and all. The next day, she wouldn't
even talk to me, and her friends yell at me for treating her
so bad. Is there something going on here I don't see?*

Signed, Just Wannabe Friends

Annie composed the answer instantly, and Mick typed:

Dear Mr. Wannabe,

Do I think there's something going on that you don't see? Do I think flies fly? Creeps creep? Ducks duck?

I'll bet that if you replayed your last few scenes with Mary, you'd see her gazing into your eyes. Did you hug her? Kiss her an oh-so-friendly kiss in the name of friendship? Right. So get real. Admit it. Something's going on. Maybe if you give your "friend" a really close look, you'll discover your friendship might be a good place to start. Ever notice that "girlfriend" has "friend" in there? Think about it.

Love, Professor Love

For her next answer, Annie dictated a list to help "eyesight" in guy-girl relationships:

Never forget that the other sex, with which you share this planet, is complex. There's almost always more going on than you think. So even if you don't have a clue to what's really going on, you'll at least be aware that you're clueless.

People aren't living in a vacuum. Don't listen to gossip, but don't ignore people's track records, either. They can only be "different" with you for so long.

Girlfriends and boyfriends should be friends, too.

Before you give in to "love at first sight," get a good pair of glasses.

Don't forget that perfect love only comes from God.

There it was again. God. Jazz let it pass and kept reading as Mick scrolled to Gracie's latest blog:

· ·
THAT'S WHAT YOU THINK!
By Jane
SUBJECT: SEEING IS BELIEVING

What you see is what you get. Right?

With this question in mind and pencil in hand, I took to the halls of Typical High this week. There, I observed a world seldom seen by the average THS student, and I noted the clues that broke the appearance barrier. Take, for example, the drama that played out in front of my locker between the Look-at-Me Kid and Prom Queen.

"I know the 'Look-at-Me Kid' has to be Bret. Who's Prom Queen?" Annie interrupted.

"Lissa Klein," Gracie answered. "But it's just a nickname. Everybody knows you're destined to be the real prom queen."

Jazz went back to the words on the screen:

The Look-at-Me Kid talked to Prom Queen, but looked at the floor, at his watch, and down the crowded hall, as if this conversation were no big deal. But these movements were jerky and screamed that they'd been rehearsed to preserve his coolness factor. But what gave him away were his hands. He preened. Three times he felt his hair or smoothed the sides of his head. That was a sure sign that the Kid liked the Queen and wanted her to like him.

The Prom Queen had her games, too. She sighed and tried to look bored. But I saw through that to the one sign that gave her away. She mimicked the Kid's hair moves. Every time he touched his hair, so did she.

Guys preen. Girls mimic. The language says, "Please like me. I like you." The clues are there, but few see.

Standing in the halls for five minutes, I observed the following: happiness, sadness, fear, anger, relief, pride, hope, disappointment, joy, hate, and even love. All there. All very, very real.

*But you can't **see** them any more than you can see the wind. Granted, you can see the signs if you're paying attention. But the things that are most real—from anger to joy, from hate to love—they're unseen.*

Mick started punching keys, and in seconds she had her verse cut and pasted at the end of Gracie's column:
So we fix our eyes not on what is seen, but on what is unseen.

For what is seen is temporary, but what is unseen is eternal.

2 Corinthians 4:18.

Jazz felt Storm's elbow poke her. "I know, Jazz. You and I aren't exactly down with these Bible things. But you have to admit this one fits."

Jazz shrugged. It fit. But that didn't mean she liked it.

12

"I still have a couple things to add to my blog," Gracie explained. "You know how our science teacher made us argue about if a tree falls in a forest and nobody's there to hear it, does it make a sound? Well, I thought I'd ask, 'If an artist paints a picture in a forest and there's nobody around to see it except the artist, is it art?'"

"Okay. Now you've got one *I* don't get," Storm admitted.

But Jazz got it. She turned to Gracie, who was staring right at her.

"How about you, Jazz?" Annie asked. "Got a cartoon yet?"

Jazz started to say no. Then she remembered what she'd doodled in art class. "Maybe. I guess it does kind of fit with the theme about not seeing things." She dug through her pack for it. She'd drawn the cartoon right after everyone *but* Gracie had complimented her fish design and Gracie had made some sarcastic crack about it. Jazz hadn't meant for her doodle to go on the site. But if the blog fit....

"Here it is." Jazz unfolded the sketch and handed it over to Mick.

Mick scanned the picture so they could all see.

The background showed a residential street in a typical suburb. All the houses on each side of the street looked exactly the same. So did the people gathered along the sides of the street and standing on their lawns, pointing. What they were pointing at was a girl, who didn't look like Gracie — Jazz wouldn't have done that — wearing a camouflage jacket that looked exactly like the one Gracie always wore. Alone, she skulked up the center of the quiet street, while the onlookers stared at her. The cloud bubble above the baffled girl read: "They can't see me. This disguise worked great in the jungle."

"I don't get it," Annie complained.

Storm, on the other hand, burst into laughter. "Annie, it's like Gracie's camouflage jacket! She may think it helps her invisible act, but it just makes her stand out."

Gracie made a point of eyeing Storm's outfit, which would have blended well in a crowd, if the crowd had been part of a circus. "Look who's talking."

Storm laughed and took a bow.

Jazz studied Gracie's face to see if she felt bad. But Gracie was smiling and telling Mick where to post the cartoon on the website.

"Can we stop now?" Annie whined. "It's Friday night. Let's do something fun!"

"Let's go see all the other fish and make fun of them because they're not as good as Jazz's!" Storm suggested.

"Aw, I don't know," Gracie said. "If you've seen one fish, you've seen 'em all."

Mick took her stepsister by the arm. "We're going, Gracie."

They left the cottage together and headed toward town. Annie and Storm talked nonstop.

"Shh! Quiet!" Jazz heard geese, their honking getting louder and louder. "Do you hear it?" The geese flew overhead in a jagged V, crossing a marbled sky that was splashed with pink by a sun trying desperately to stay above the horizon. Closer to ground, sky blue mixed with gray and came out purple. In the expanse, eight shades of blue swirled behind the pink-striped background. "Isn't it something?" Jazz whispered.

Mick was the closest one to her. "The heavens declare the glory of God," she said softly, gazing up at the sky. "The skies proclaim the work of his hands." She smiled at Jazz. "Psalm 19:1."

Another Bible verse. Jazz should have been irritated. But she wasn't.

Mick had picked up a map of the fish entries, and she led the troops to the book store on Highway 42 first, where a woman had painted a shiny silvery fish and labeled it "Perch." It was a decent job, although not very colorful. Jazz glanced at it, then turned around to stare at the giant maple across the street. She wondered how many decades it had taken that tree to get so powerful. The roots had exploded through the ground, cracking the sidewalk into dozens of jagged lines.

Jazz loved Big Lake's old, broken sidewalks, the way they rolled, like boiling oatmeal. Those roots told a story about the triumph of the trees. Even tiny blades of grass, or dandelions, could push through cracks in a sidewalk, some of them forcing their way through concrete a breath at a time.

She followed along with her friends on the grand fish tour, but she barely saw the other statues. She was too captivated by the way mud had formed rain-splattered patterns in the street they crossed. Or the tangle of weeds around a stop sign. Or the concentric lines of stomped-out cigarette butts piled into gravel at the corner of Crafts-R-Us, where Paul's bass lay in the window as if all the fight had drained out of it.

They ended the fish tour at Sam's Sammich Shop and gazed in at the largemouth bass.

"No contest," Storm pronounced. "Yours is so much better than everybody's, Jazz."

Jazz stared at the fish, *her* fish that didn't feel at all like hers. This largemouth bass had nothing to say. That's why the legend board was blank. It was speechless.

"Don't you still need to write something on the white board there, besides your name?" Annie asked.

"I can't do it," Jazz said.

"We can help you come up with something," Storm offered.

Jazz shook her head. "Not that. The fish. I can't enter this fish."

"What are you talking about?" Storm cried. "You've got first place locked."

Jazz turned to Gracie. A smile was playing at the corners of Gracie's mouth.

"I can't do this!" Jazz laughed. She felt as if a heavy blanket had been lifted off her shoulders. Or maybe it felt more like swimming up from the bottom of a big lake and bursting above the surface of the water. She could breathe again.

Jazz raced inside, and the others followed her. The shop wasn't that busy for a Friday night. "Sam!" she shouted.

Samantha Lind waved from behind the counter. "What's up?"

Jazz rushed over to her. She nodded to Mr. Hamilton, Hamlet, who was sitting on one of the stools. His hair was getting long, pushing at the turtleneck of his brown cable-knit sweater. "Could I stay here after you close?" Jazz begged. "I won't hurt anything. I promise. I need to work on my fish."

"I thought you were finished, Jazz," Sam said.

Jazz shook her head. "I've barely started. Please?"

"Well, sure. You'll have to close up when you're finished, though."

"I have a feeling it's going to take me all night."

Sam frowned. "I don't know about letting you spend the whole night here by yourself, Jazz."

"I'll stay with her." Annie walked up and sat on the stool next to Hamlet.

"You don't have to, Annie. This is my job."

"Me too!" Storm shouted.

"I'll call Mom and see if it's okay for me to spend the night," Mick chimed in. "And we can finish the shift for you, Sam, so you could go home early."

"We'll cover breakfast, too," Annie offered. "You can sleep in. We'll have a sleepover!"

Jazz turned to Gracie.

Gracie grinned. "Count me in."

"Great!" Jazz said. "'Cause I can use all of you. We've got so much work to do!"

They called their parents and got permission. Then Annie drove everybody home for sleeping bags and overnight stuff.

When they got back, Hamlet offered to drive Annie's mom home so a car could stay behind at the shop.

Jazz sent Gracie to the hardware store for sandpaper and cotton masks while Annie and Mick served the last customers and closed up. Then they all reported to Jazz for duty.

"Here's the deal," she explained. "I can't just paint over the fish because it wouldn't dry in time for me to paint on a new design. So we'll have to sand off the paint."

"Are you sure you want to do this?" Storm asked, staring at the fish like she was saying good-bye to an old friend.

"Are you kidding?" Jazz replied. "It's the first thing I've been sure of all week."

It took them four hours to sand down the fish. Then they kept going until every last mark of the design was gone.

"My fingers will never be the same," Annie said, examining her nails.

Mick was nodding off, sandpaper in hand.

"You guys better get some sleep," Jazz said. "Don't worry. I don't need anybody to keep me going. I couldn't sleep if I wanted to."

Half an hour later the others had fallen asleep in sleeping bags lined up across the floor. Jazz stood in the window, the only overhead light pointing down on the fish, and she painted. Really painted this time. She couldn't work fast enough. It felt as if her fingers moved the brushes without her, forming lines for her to trail after. The movement itself excited her, the lines falling into the right places, making a sea of air, forming a story, a narrative about a fish born to be out of water. But the fish swam in water anyway, until it sank so low that it couldn't breathe at the bottom of the lake.

Then it saw. It saw what no other fish had ever seen — a world beyond, above, an invisible world. And the fish believed. It chose to believe in the unseen because what was up there felt more real than what was down at the bottom of the lake.

Jazz felt something else, too. A presence that seemed closer than if someone had been standing next to her. Another creator? *The* Creator? The scenes that flew through her mind included honking geese, maple trees, roots that cracked through concrete walks — all astounding creations. Mick's verse was right. Everything she saw, the beauty that was everywhere, it all proclaimed the work of God's hands.

Red, yellow, and green lines rose and fell, then soared to the top of the fish's fin, as the fish flew out of the water and into the new world. The fish's mouth burst with words, truths to tell anyone who would listen. The mouth grew larger and larger, its message louder and louder. And Jazz heard the message. God was the Creator. Of course. God had made everything Jazz loved. The seen and the unseen. She couldn't pretend any longer that he wasn't there, not when she saw him everywhere.

Light peeked through the front window when Gracie climbed out of her sleeping bag and joined Jazz by her fish. Gracie walked around the fish, examining it from all sides. "Now that's art."

They stared at it together, as Gracie kept talking. "It's totally spun, Jazz! I can feel the joy in this fish. A discovery, right? It's like the fish wants to talk and tell us something."

"Yeah!" Jazz wasn't sure she could have said it any better. "This is the fish I saw all along, even when I tried to paint the other one. You really see it, don't you, Gracie?"

"So do you, Jazz," Gracie said. "I've never met anybody more in tune with the 'unseen' than you are. There's no way you can't believe in God. He's an artist, like you."

Jazz couldn't stop grinning. There was too much beauty in even the garbage and cigarette butts, not to mention the trees and the sky. "I know," she whispered. "I know." There was a lot she wanted to learn. She felt that she was beginning a journey, a narrative, her own story, and she'd just taken the first step.

Without any trouble at all, Jazz wrote the legend of her fish and dedicated it to DC:

Fish Out of Water

By Jasmine Fletcher

This Fish-Out-of-Water suffered in the Big Lake, trying to be like the other fish at the bottom of the lake. But then he began a great journey. He believed in an unseen world, where he could soar into waves of air that no one in the lake could see. His journey led him into an unseen world that was more real than anything he saw at the bottom of the lake. And the unseen best of this world — joy, trust, love, God — live on eternally.

I dedicate this fish to the memory of DC, who lives in another world, a world the rest of us can't see now, where nobody hurts and nobody dies.

Next to the legend, she tacked one of Kendra's drawings, one she'd made for her brother.

"It's perfect, Jazz," Gracie said.

"Thanks."

"You do know that you're going to lose the fish competition now."

"Yep."

"Congratulations."

13

Gracie and Jazz took over the kitchen at Sam's Sammich Shop, and the smell of bacon woke everybody up. They rolled out of their sleeping bags and ran over to check out the new fish.

"Sweet! Those colors are filled with grooviness!" Storm shouted.

"It's cool, Jazz!" Mick exclaimed. "I'm not sure what it is, but I can't stop looking at it. I don't know much about art, but I'll bet this is it."

"Thanks, Mick." Jazz wanted to say something to Mick about the verse. She'd been pretty hard on her about posting verses on the blog. She'd do it later, when she got Mick by herself. There'd be time. She had a feeling she was in for a long journey of little steps.

"Kickin' title!" Annie offered. "That's the best title out of everybody's. Plus, nobody will get your fish mixed up with the other fishes."

"Thanks, Annie."

They got cleaned up and ready for the breakfast crowd. It really was a crowd, with people out to see the public art contest. It was almost funny to watch the expressions on people's faces as they saw the all-new fish. Annie had assigned Jazz kitchen duties, and Jazz had a feeling it was to spare her from hearing the fish debate going on out front. But Jazz still managed to catch some of it.

"What happened to the bass?" a man asked. "The real fish?"

"This is the real fish," Gracie answered.

"That other one looked like a real bass," he countered.

"Maybe," Gracie admitted. "But this one is art. Go on. Take a really good look at it. It's a story wrapped up in a fish."

The man stared at the fish. He walked to the other side and stared some more. "You know what? I used to talk about that big one what got away, when we used to fish the waters to the north. Got to be a joke between my dad and me. I'll betcha this is that fish. Makes me remember...." He stood and stared at it for a full minute, then nodded slowly and took his seat.

Gracie made each customer look, really look, at the fish. Not all of them got it. But a few did. They tried to guess what the fish had to tell them. And each story was different, yet somehow the same.

"They're coming!" Storm shouted. "The judges!"

Jazz peeked from behind the counter and saw two men and a woman, all in business suits, huddled together outside the picture window. They frowned and scribbled on their clipboards. They didn't even bother to come in.

Judging ended by noon, and the results were supposed to be posted at City Hall. Jazz had no desire to go and look at the list, so Storm and Mick ran over to see who won. When they came back, it didn't take a genius to figure out that Jazz hadn't placed.

"Sorry, Jazz," Mick offered. "Paul got an honorable mention."

Jazz knew Paul would be disappointed, but at least his fish would probably make some money in the auction. Hers would likely end up in the trash. So far, not a single silent bid had been placed by her fish.

"You okay?" Gracie asked.

"I'm okay. I won't have a studio in my house, but I'm okay." Funny, but she meant it. She'd given up her studio. She'd forfeited any chance she'd had at winning the business proposition and a little respect from the 'rents. But it was worth it to be off of the bottom of the lake and at the beginning of a journey she hadn't dreamed possible before all this happened.

They kept the shop running until Sam showed up with Annie's grandparents to take over. Then they left for the cottage because none of them felt like sticking around for the results of the silent auction since Jazz's fish still didn't have a bid.

At the cottage, Jazz stretched out on the couch. The next thing she knew, the phone made her jerk awake. It took her a second to remember where she was.

"It's your cell!" Storm shouted.

Jazz tried to focus. She flipped open the cover on her phone and checked the time. She'd been asleep for three hours.

Her mother was on the line. "Are you okay, Jasmine?"

"I'm fine."

"I heard about the contest. I'm sorry yours didn't win."

"Yeah. Me too. Listen, I'll be home in a little while, okay?"

"Jasmine, your father needs to see you."

"Okay then."

"What do they know?" Storm asked. "They picked the fish at the university. I can't even remember what it looked like."

"Not at home. He's at work. He asked if you could stop by Spiels to see him."

"At work?" Jazz couldn't remember the last time she'd gone by the office. "Dad wants me to go by Spiels? Why?" She frowned at Annie and Storm, who were staring at her.

"Will you just do it, Jasmine? I can come give you a ride if you need one."

"I can take you," Annie whispered.

Jazz smiled thanks at Annie. "Mom, Annie said she'd give me a lift."

"Good. All right then. I'll see you when you get home."

"Why do you have to go to your dad's office?" Storm asked after Jazz had hung up.

"I have no idea." But then she got it. "Oh man! I'll bet he heard about the contest, that I'm a big loser, and he's going to make me apply for that Christmas internship at Spiels! Can you believe them? It's only been a couple of hours since I lost. Rub it in, why don't they?"

Everybody rode along to give Jazz moral support. Annie's old car looked out of place in the Spiel's parking lot, filled with BMW's and Volvos and power cars.

"Thanks, guys," Jazz said. "You don't have to wait. Really. I can catch a ride home with Dad."

"Are you kidding?" Storm asked, taking off her seatbelt. "We're coming in with you."

The others unbuckled their belts, too, and started getting out.

"Are you sure? This probably isn't going to be pretty. I'm not going down without a fight."

"Pretty is in the eye of the beholder," Gracie said. "Now walk."

They had to go through security to enter the seven-story office building. Mick led the way through the marbled-floor entry. She stopped. "Jazz! Come here! Look at this!"

Jazz caught up with Mick and looked where she was pointing. Across the entry, in front of giant fountain, was her fish. Jazz blinked to be sure she wasn't imagining it. Then she saw her dad coming down the stairs on the other side of the hall. She ran over to him.

They stood a few feet away from her fish, and both of them stared at it.

"How did that get here? I mean, it's my fish, Dad."

Her dad smiled at the fish. "I know. I like it a lot better than that other fish, too."

"You do?"

"There's just something about it, Jasmine. I don't know what it is, but I like it. I paid good money for it, too."

"You're kidding?"

He shook his head. "That's the trouble with a silent auction. You have to bid high."

"You paid money for my fish? Does Mom know?"

"She was there with me, Jasmine. I liked what I saw even before I read the legend ... and the dedication. But I love what you wrote for DC. So does your mother."

Jazz glanced through the fountain at her friends, clustered together where she'd left them. They looked like they were getting ready to come to her rescue.

"Dad bought my fish!" Jazz shouted.

Her friends cheered, and their cheers echoed in the halls of Spiels Corporation.

She'd lost the contest. But her whole world had opened up. And God was in that world. She didn't know much more than that, except that God was probably the most real thing in the world. How could that be losing? *Thank you, God.* The prayer formed itself in her heart, and she said it again.

Jazz's eyes were watering, but she could see the pieces of her life coming together, the way the pieces of her art did when she painted. With her art, she had always sensed that her creation had existed somewhere already and she was simply unraveling it, figuring out where the pieces fit onto the canvas.

That's how it felt now. It was as if Someone, a great Creator, had known all along this is where she'd be, at the start of her journey. She was stepping out, believing in an unseen God she did not know, but with the promise that she wouldn't be alone on the journey anymore.

Internet Safety by Michaela

People aren't always what they seem at first, like wolves in sheep's clothing. Chat rooms, blogs, and other places online can be fun ways to meet all kinds of people with all kinds of interests. But be aware and cautious. Here are some tips to help keep you safe while surfing the web, keeping a blog, chatting online, and writing emails.

- Never give out personal information such as your address, phone number, parents' work addresses or phone numbers, or the name and address of your school without your parents' or guardian's permission. It's okay to talk about your likes and dislikes, but keep private information just that—private.

- Before you agree to meet someone in person, first check with your parents or guardian to make sure it's okay. A safe way to meet for the first time is to bring a parent or guardian with you.

- You might be tempted to send a picture of yourself to new friends you've met online. Just in case your acquaintance is not who you think they are, check with your parent or guardian before you hit send.

- If you feel uncomfortable by angry, threatening, or other types of emails or posts addressed to you, tell your parent or guardian immediately.

- Before you promise to call a new friend on the telephone, talk to your parent or guardian first.

- Remember that just because you might read about something or someone online doesn't mean the information is true. Sometimes people say cruel or untruthful things just to be mean.

- If someone writes creepy posts, report him or her to the blog or website owner.

Following these tips will help keep you safe while you hang out online. If you're careful, you can learn a lot and meet tons of new people.

Subject: Michaela Jenkins

Age: 13 on May 19, 7th grade at Big Lake Middle School
Hair/Eyes: Dark brown hair/Brown eyes
Height: 5'

"Mick the Munch" is content and rooted in her relationship with Christ. She lives with her step-sis, Grace Doe, in the blended family of Gracie's dad and Mick's mom. She's a tomboy, an avid Cleveland Indians fan, and the only girl on her school's baseball team. A computer whiz, Mick keeps *That's What You Think!* up and running. She also helps out at Sam's Sammich Shop and manages to show her friends what deep faith looks like.

Subject: Grace Doe

Age: 15 on August 19, sophomore
Hair/Eyes: Blonde hair/Hazel eyes
Height: 5', 5"

Grace doesn't think she is cute at all. The word "average" was meant for her. She dresses in neutral colors and camouflage to blend in. Grace does not wear makeup. She prefers to observe life rather than participate in it. A bagger at a grocery store, only her close friends and family can get away with calling her "Gracie." She is part of a blended family and lives with Dad and step-mom, two step-siblings, and two half brothers. Her mother's job frequently keeps her out of town.

Subject: Annie Lind

Age: 16 on October 1, sophomore
Hair/Eyes: Auburn hair/Blue eyes
Height: 5', 10"

Annie desperately wants guys to admire and like her. She is boy-crazy and thinks she always has to be in love. She considers herself to be an expert in matters of the heart. Annie takes being popular for granted because she has always been well-liked. She loves and admires her mom. Her dad was killed in a plane crash when Annie was two months old. Annie helps out at Sam's Sammich Shop, her mom's restaurant. She can be self-centered, though without being selfish.

Subject: Jasmine Fletcher

Age: 15 on July 13, freshman
Hair/Eyes: Black hair/Brown eyes
Height: 5', 6"

Jasmine is an artist who feels that no one, especially her art teacher and parents, understands her art. She is African American, and has great fashion sense, without being trendy. Her parents are quite well-to-do, and they won't let Jasmine get a job. She has a younger brother and a sister who has Down syndrome. She also had a brother who was killed in a drive-by shooting in the old neighborhood when Jazz was one.

Subject: Storm Novello

Age: 14 on September 1, freshman
Hair/Eyes: Brown hair/Dark brown eyes
Height: 5', 2"

Storm doesn't realize how pretty she is. She wishes she had blonde hair. She is Mayan/Mestisa, and claims to be a Mayan princess. Storm always needs to be the center of attention and doesn't let on how smart she is. She dresses in bright, flouncy clothing, and wears too much makeup. Storm is a completely different person around her parents. She changes into her clothes and puts her makeup on after leaving for school. Her parents are very loving, though they have little money.

1

Storm Novelo stared at the computer screen. It was Saturday morning, and she should have been at the mall. Or better yet, still in bed. Anywhere, except here at Gracie's mother's cottage, blogging for the website.

"Might as well get typing," Annie Lind suggested. "We're not letting you out of the room until you finish your column." Even in her jogging suit, Annie had style. Shoulder-length auburn hair framed her giant blue eyes and tiny nose.

"I still can't believe you guys would kidnap a person just because she's a little late with her trivia column," Storm complained. "Isn't there a law against kidnapping?"

Okay, so she was two weeks late on her contribution to *That's What You Think*. Big deal.

Annie turned a page of her teen magazine. Usually, she was late with her "Professor Love" advice column. Only not today. She was totally chizzlin', sprawled by the window, her long legs dangling over the arm of the big white chair. Storm figured her own legs wouldn't have dangled at all. At five-ten, Annie was a good eight inches taller than Storm.

"Don't know about that kidnapping law," Annie said. "But according to Gracie, there *is* a law against being late with your column."

That's What You Think had been Grace Doe's idea all the
way. She'd been blogging her observations a long time before
she got the rest of the team on board. Gracie had a way of
reading people by observing subtle gestures and signs. In the
beginning, Storm had thought being part of a website group
rocked. But now she was getting bored with it, like she did
with everything. At least this project had lasted longer than
most. And she'd made some great friends in the process.
Gracie, Annie, Jazz, and Mick — the other members of the
blog team — were as good of friends as Storm ever got. Better.

While she formatted her page, Storm thought back to her
first impressions of Big Lake, Ohio. This time her dad's end-
less search for lawn-care jobs had taken them to a town with
no lake, in spite of the name, and a skyline that offered nothing but trees and a water tower. Still, something about the
town had felt right.

It might have been because the whole town, especially Big
Lake High School, where Storm enrolled as a freshman,
seemed so familiar. As it turned out, the school *was* familiar.
Before the move, Storm had been reading dozens of web
logs. She thought of them as open diaries on the Internet.
Her favorite blog had been *That's What You Think* by someone
calling herself "Jane." Jane wrote about a school she dubbed
"Typical High."

Once Storm started attending classes at Big Lake High
School, it hadn't taken her long to figure out that "Typical
High" was actually Big Lake High and Grace Doe, a
sophomore at BLHS, was "Jane." Storm and Gracie had
gotten off to a rough start. But in the end, Gracie had invited
her to join the blog team. Storm's job was to write a column

called "Didyanose," as in "Did You Know?" She just wrote trivia, spilling out some of the facts that rolled around in her head all the time. At first, she'd loved having an outlet for her trivia because it cut down on her too-smart-sounding outbursts in classes. But lately, the whole thing had definitely been getting old.

Case in point: this week's column on body image. Writing facts about the human body should have been a snap. Storm knew thousands of facts and lots of trivia about the body. She could spout them off the top of her head. She read everything — encyclopedias, hospital brochures, bulletin boards, medical sites on the Internet. She couldn't help herself. She even read cereal boxes, car instruction manuals, labels on household cleaning products, and the fine print on everything. Her parents didn't understand, and they never would.

"Finished yet, Storm?" Gracie strolled from the kitchen, munching on a bagel that smelled like it had peanut butter on it.

"Getting there," Storm answered. "But don't try to read over my shoulder or I'll never get it. Anyway, shouldn't we be going to the supermarket?" She and Gracie worked as baggers at Big Lake Foods, although Storm was seriously considering quitting. She was tired of bagging groceries and making small talk with customers, even though she'd loved the job at first.

"You have two hours before your shift starts, Storm," Gracie said, taking a big bite of bagel. "Use them."

"So where's Jazz?" Storm asked, stalling.

"She's already turned in her cartoon," Gracie explained, not taking the bait. "And in case you're wondering, Mick's coming by after practice so she can upload *all* of our columns to the site."

Mick, Gracie's little stepsister, was the computer genius who kept the website running. She was also the only girl on the Big Lake Middle School baseball team.

As soon as Gracie went upstairs, Storm did a computer search until she found Gracie's latest blog. This was their second blog on the "body" because they'd gotten so many great emails after the first one. Storm leaned back in the computer chair and read:

· ·
THAT'S WHAT YOU THINK!
By Jane
NOVEMBER 3
SUBJECT: YOU

Does every female wear a size 2? Or is it just that they all get to appear on TV, and we think that's the norm? Where are those TV censors when you really need them? I think we should all write our local stations and have them ban the airwaves carrying programs in which TV actresses wear anything smaller than a 9 or 10.

Did it ever occur to them that we weren't all supposed to have the same body? Just imagine what life would be like if all girls were slim and shapely and every guy was all buff and muscle-bound. Oh — and we all had great hair. Then how would we know who was more desirable? Who to make homecoming king and queen? Who to envy? We'd have to make up other things — like who had the straightest toes, or the thickest eyebrows or something. If only we worried that much about our insides.

At Typical High today, in one 5-minute period between classes, I observed 22 hair checks. I heard 2 girls ask the fat question: "Do you think this makes me look fat?" And I observed 3 guys making a gorilla attempt to thrust out their chests when a size 2 girl strolled by.

On the other hand, accepting your body doesn't necessarily mean flaunting it. Why does every girl feel she has to wear those short, belly-revealing tops, when 90% of us would like for that little roll of fat to be invisible?

Storm skimmed the rest of the rant. As usual, Mick had posted a Bible verse after Gracie's column:

You knit me together in my mother's womb. I praise you because I am fearfully and wonderfully made. (Psalm 139:13, 14)

Most days Storm believed that — that God actually created everybody. Her parents went to church service every week, but they didn't make Storm go anymore.

She had to hunt for Jazz's latest cartoon, but she finally found the scanned-in copy, ready to be uploaded to the site. It was a picture of a clown, with a little boy biting the clown's hand. The word balloon above the boy's head read, "Huh. He doesn't taste funny." The thought balloon over the clown's head said, "Everybody's a critic."

Storm laughed and then skimmed through Annie's advice column. Annie had taken a different angle this time, and Storm suspected it was because "Professor Love" got so much mail. Usually, Annie only answered a couple of questions, but this time, she'd answered a bunch of them — all with one liners:

·
THAT'S WHAT YOU THINK!

Dear Professor Love,

I adore my boyfriend, but our relationship is so not fair! I work out and hardly eat anything. I get so bummed when I see the littlest bit of fat. But he eats whatever he wants, and he doesn't care if he's kind of . . . well, chubby. I don't think he even notices when he's the worst-dressed person at a party. How can guys be like that? When we're so super aware of how we look to them, how can they just go along like everything's great? How can they be so happy?

— Baffled

Dear Baffled,

Because ignorance is bliss.

Love, Professor Love

Dear Professor Love,

I love my girlfriend, and I want her 2 have a good time. So I take her 2 all kinds of parties. But she finds something wrong @ every party. Either the right people aren't there, or it's 2 loud, or it's 2 dead, or there's nothing 2 do, or they want her 2 do 2 much. Tell me how 2 make these parties better.

— Partyboy

Dear Partyboy,

Ask your girlfriend to leave said parties.

Love, Professor Love

Dear Professor Love,

I'm trying to help this guy I'm dating eat right and have a healthy lifestyle. But all he wants to do is cruise fast-food windows and down burgers. What can I do to help him achieve a balanced diet??

— Healthnut

Dear Healthnut,

To him, it is a "balanced diet — a burger in each hand.

Love, Professor Love

Dear Professor Love,

What's the big deal about having a girlfriend? I'm a player and proud of it! I date a different girl each night, man! If you took one look at me, you'd know why. I could have any woman I please.

— Player

Dear Player,

Too bad you haven't pleased any.

Love, Professor Love

Dear Professor Love,

This guy I like can't shut up in class. He still throws spit-wads at other guys and does stuff like we did in elementary school. Why do you think he acts like such an idiot?

— Puzzled

Dear Puzzled,

Who says he's acting?

Love, Professor Love

At the end of her column, Annie had added something new — her own little blog about love:

Dear Readers, as you know, Professor Love always goes for the laugh. But I wouldn't be doing my job if I didn't toss out something serious for you to think about while you're going through problems of the heart. So, here it is: Try to look past the cover of the book and start reading the actual book.

The front door slammed, and Storm looked up as Jazz and Mick rushed in together.

Storm swiveled to face them. Mick's jeans looked like she'd slid into home. Her brown ponytail stuck out of her Cleveland Indian's baseball cap. Jazz's black jeans and sweatshirt probably cost more than anything in Storm's closet, but Storm knew Jazz didn't care about clothes.

"Hey, guys!" Storm called. "Thought you'd never get here."

faThGirLz!™
2 corinthians 4:18

Inner Beauty, Outward Faith

Sophie's World
(Book 1)
0-310-70756-0

Sophie's Secret
(Book 2)
0-310-70757-9

Sophie and the Scoundrels
(Book 3)
0-310-70758-7

Sophie's Irish
Showdown (Book 4)
0-310-70759-5

Sophie's First Dance?
(Book 5)
0-310-70760-9

Sophie's Stormy
Summer (Book 6)
0-310-70761-7

Sophie Breaks
the Code (Book 7)
0-310-71022-7

Sophie Tracks a Thief
(Book 8)
0-310-71023-5

Sophie Flakes Out
(Book 9)
0-310-71024-3

Sophie Loves Jimmy
(Book 10)
0-310-71025-1

Sophie Loses the Lead
(Book 11)
0-310-71026-X

Sophie's Encore
(Book 12)
0-310-71027-8

Available now at your local bookstore!

faiThGirLz!
2 corinthians 4:18

Inner Beauty, Outward Faith

With TNIV text and Faithgirlz™ sparkle, this Bible goes right to the heart of a girl's world and has a unique landscape format perfect for sharing.

The Faithgirlz™ TNIV Bible • Hardcover • 0-310-71002-2

The Faithgirlz™ TNIV Bible • Faux Fur • 0-310-71004-9

Available now at your local bookstore!

zonder**kidz**

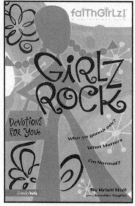

faiThGirLz!
2 corinthians 4:18

Inner Beauty, Outward Faith

Now available from **inspirio**

Faithgirlz!™ Bible Cover
Large ISBN 0-310-80780-8
Medium ISBN 0-310-80781-6

Faithgirlz!™ CD Case
ISBN 0-310-81137-6

Faithgirlz!™ Backpack
ISBN 0-310-81228-3

Available now at your local bookstore!

faiThGirLz!

2 corinthians 4:18

Inner Beauty, Outward Faith

Visit **faithgirlz.com**—
it's the place for girls ages 8-12!